praise for Michael Guillebeau

praise for DON OF THE Q

"*Don of the Q* is highly recommended as an original, involving read that pushes the boundaries of comedy, stormy relationships, and social commentary alike."

— *D. Donovan, Senior Reviewer, Midwest Book Review*

"A much-needed book in these times…entertaining…and the message is compelling."

— *Risah Salazaar, Reader's Favorite*

"Straight to the heart of the truth, without any clothes on the Emperor himself... Love it!"

—*Li Tian, PhD, author of WESTBOUND: A MEMOIR: MY JOURNEY FROM BEIJING TO NEW YORK CITY praise for MAD LIBRARIAN (2017 Foreword Reviews Humor Book of the Year)*

"Guillebeau (*Josh Whoever*) blends humor and mystery perfectly in this comic thriller set in the small city of Maddington, Ala. . . .Guillebeau keeps things light with frequent laugh-out-loud lines."
—*Publisher's Weekly*

praise for JOSH WHOEVER (Library Journal Mystery Debut of the Month)

"…the collection of oddball minor characters and surprise twists deepen an already strong story. …An engrossing debut."
—*Library Journal*

Don of the Q

An American Don Quixote for the Atomic Age

by Michael Guillebeau

Madison Press
Madison, Alabama

This is a work of fiction. Names, characters, places, and incidents are a product of the author's imagination. Locales and public names are sometimes used for atmospheric purposes. Any resemblance to actual people, living or dead, or to businesses, companies, events, institutions, or locales is completely coincidental.

Published by Madison Press
Madison, Alabama
madisonpresspublishing@gmail.com

Book Layout © 2017 BookDesignTemplates.com
Cover Design by www.ruslan.us.
PRE07202020

Don of the Q/ Michael Guillebeau. – 1st ed.
PB ISBN: 978-0-9972055-7-2
EBOOK ISBN: 978-0-9972055-6-5

day one: 2:00 p.m.

the world blinks

The world blinks and is gone. For a second of total darkness, it is as if nothing has ever existed for me before this moment.

I blink back, and the convenience store world slowly emerges: newborn lights, rows of cans stacked on convenience store shelves and a steel counter in front of me, all strange but somehow familiar. One blur steps forward, grows color, shape, and becomes a man in front of me.

The words come out of me without thought. "I don't know what I'm doing here."

He slams a six-pack of our cheapest beer on the counter between us.

"Very funny, asshole. You're here to overcharge me. Same as yesterday."

"Three dollars and thirty-four cents," I say. Don't know how I know this, but there it is.

Pointing, he says, "You're supposed to use that."

Where he's pointing, a gray blur resolves itself into a cash register with the Quick Stop logo on it. At my back is a white, wooden lifeguard's chair.

It seems odd. Why would anyone want to sit there?

He leans across the counter, spitting in my face now. "Three goddamned dollars and thirty-four goddamn cents. You say you don't know why you're here, and I say I don't know why I let you and your boss charge me so much for the essentials of life." He is a big man, rough, dirty; used to getting in other people's faces. "Much money as I've spent in here, this damned well ought to be free."

Maybe this is my purpose here. "Take it, bro." I smile, proud to add a momentary exchange of sunlight to the semi-darkness of the convenience store cave. I give him generosity; he will give me thanks. We will go on with our day brightened by a positive moment with a stranger who is now a friend. "With blessings."

The store is in perpetual twilight, but the customer and I stand like two glowing beings under the counter light. I smile bigger. My kindness seems to perfect the charming image, and I'm sure this is why I'm here.

His stare turns to contempt. "Rip your boss off, boy? No goddamned loyalty anymore." He reaches across me and takes a handful of Slim Jims. "Taking these, too." At the door, he turns back and spits on the floor. "Goddamned foreigners."

The doorbell tinkles like it must have when he came in. Maybe that's what triggered my memory loss. Maybe not. I look around and the inside of the store snaps into clarity. Missing light bulbs, dark patches, dirty floors, and shelves of bright-colored products. I know the price of everything.

It's all clear now, except why I'm here. Maybe I am a foreigner. But something's going on here.

day one: 3:00 p.m.

there was a crooked man

Left alone, cleaning up seems like the thing to do. I'm sweeping the floor and humming an old rock song when Sancha comes in and I give her a quick smile. She gives me a bored jerk of the head. I guess we don't have a smiling kind of relationship. I put on a bored look to match hers.

"Who lit a fire under your ass?" She points her chin at the broom and dumps a load of textbooks onto the one bare spot on the counter between lighters and mega-caffeine pills. "First time I ever seen you do anything more than you have to." She pauses and grunts. "First time I seen anybody here do any more than we have to."

"Seemed like the thing to do," I say, but I lean the broom against the wall. I wonder how I know Sancha's name but don't know I'm not supposed to sweep up. I give up and decide I know what I know and don't know what I don't. Sancha shuffles behind the counter and flips open one of her books.

"Sancha, we're pretty tight, right?"

She looks up, startled. "You're a mean, crooked little twist of a twenty-something acting like an old man sitting shriveled up in his high throne there every day. Yell at the customers and me without saying anything coherent, except that you hate us all. I have the bad luck to see you for the thirty seconds it takes you to clear out of the Q when I take over for the evening shift. Don't know your family or friends, or even if you've got any."

She drops the book back on the pile.

"But, yeah, that means you're probably the best friend I got." She thinks about that a minute and puts her head down on the counter. "My life sucks."

"I need to ask you something, for real," I say. "I don't know who I am or what I'm doing here."

She looks at me and snorts. "You and me both, Don. You and me both."

"No, I mean . . . not like that. It's like it's a new day and I can't even remember the old days. And there are voices in my head, like from God or something, saying 'Who you are is what you settle for,' you know?"

"That's not God, man. That was Janis Joplin, old classic blues singer, that said that. Are you back to your old man self now?"

"I don't know. I mean I know my name. But I mean. . . the guy who was just in here called me a foreigner. Am I a foreigner?"

She squints.

"I don't know, man. I always thought you were white. But I guess I can see what he meant. You're kind of dark-skinned. Sort of. I don't know, man. You're just one of those guys that nobody notices one way or another. And I think that "foreigner" is just one of those words some people like to spit out at the world these days." She laughs. "What the hell do I know? A half-black, half-Chicano queer chick like me, everybody looks white."

I can see I'm not going to get any more answers, so I leave. I think about taking a drink and a Slim Jim, just grab them like the guy did earlier. I don't think Sancha would stop me. But something feels wrong about that, so I don't.

I stop at the taco truck next door, rusting white with orange and green words in Spanish and misspelled English. A small dark man in the truck hands me a *tacos de pollo adobado* as if he knows I get it every day. He smiles and overcharges me, and I smile back and walk away.

Walking down Triana Boulevard toward home I realize that I know how to get home, but everything else here seems new to me. I see—like I know I've seen every day—the sagging porches and rotten wood of the hundred-year-old duplexes and the old men slumped on porches like piles of pent-up helpless rage. But today the bright afternoon sunshine pumps life into a neighbor-hood grown dark and I imagine—no, I see—roses bloom pink and yellow and reach for the sun. Fresh, clean paint flows up walls like magic and real neighbors start to laugh together, and it looks like a beautiful place. I look around and take a bite of my dinner as I walk. The taco is hotter than the sun on this hot Alabama summer day and I wish I had taken a beer. But the taste is fire-bright and clean, like the neighborhood I see in my mind today. I take another bite, and another.

Grease and sauce are running down my chin as I pass a crumbling storefront with dirty windows and a hand-painted sign that reads, BROTHERHOOD OF GOD. A smiling man on the sidewalk tracks me with his eyes.

"God wants you, brother," he says as I pass. I stop and smile back and wonder if he knows why I'm here. He hands me a wad of tissues.

"Lot of tears in this neighborhood, son," he says. "I keep the tissue box out for folks who need them. These tissues will be grateful for the chance to soak up some hot sauce instead." He motions to my chin and I clean myself up. A phone rings somewhere in the church behind him and he smiles again.

"That's my call." He goes inside and I go on home, wondering who or what's on the other end of the line.

There's a small house that I know is mine, but I see it fresh now. It is tiny, probably built as a shed for the sagging duplex next door, then converted with a few sheets of plywood into a rental. Can't rent for much if a clerk from the Q can afford it. But it is neat and tidy and cared for. I put the key in the door and walk in.

day one: 4:00 p.m.

people and purpose

Everything inside my house comforts me and I understand what the expression "feeling at home" means. There's a big soft chair, just one, in front of the TV. When I sit down, the floor creaks like it's going to give in, but it doesn't. I turn the TV on.

On screen, a stylish twenty-something woman in a business suit stands over a girl's dead body. The body is horribly mutilated, but the school uniform and textbooks tell the woman that the victim was probably a local student on her way home after class. The woman flirts with a hot alpha-male guy in an Armani suit. He makes a wry but sensitive comment while staring at the sun. Heavy rock music swells as the opening credits roll.

I'm shocked. Is this real, maybe happening down the street? What will they do about the dead girl? I sit in front of the TV throughout the evening. Before my eyes flutter closed, I count seventeen murders, and I can remember every one. I look around my comforting little house and can't see how it is part of the world I have just watched.

I go to bed and hope that I'll dream of my house, or maybe tacos, but I don't. I dream of a line of people stumbling numb toward me, like zombies. The first TV victim, the young girl, comes at me with her face melted. Behind her are her parents, an angry old man from the neighborhood, more people, so many I can't count. The line stretches up the street from my house to the convenience store, to the highway, maybe forever, each person angrier and more damaged by the world.

Something pulls at my shoulder and the preacher floats in front of my face.

"God wants you, brother," he says.

I wake up gasping. My breath comes to me slow, like a first breath. Right now, staring into the sunrise, I realize why I am here. I don't know what Sancha thought I was yesterday, but today I know: I am an angel sent here on a mission. I can go home to heaven when I've fulfilled my quest.

day two: 6:00 a.m.

royals

The late-shift guy, Atlas, is shocked when I come in an hour early for the day shift.

"Take off, bro," I say. "I'm supposed to be here."

"You sure?"

"Very sure." I smile just a little, careful that I don't smile too big and light up the store with my new heavenly presence and give my mission away. Now I understand why Mary and the saints are always painted with little half-smiles instead of big grins.

"Gonna get paid for my whole shift?" he says.

"I'll clock you out later. You'll get paid." He's out of here before my words finish echoing. The power of an angel's command.

Through the glass, I see a guy in his twenties and a woman a little younger huddled on the sidewalk. The man is doing the talking, gesturing and pleading, while the woman is curled up, head down, arms around her knees. The sun's just starting to take full command of the day. I take two cardboard cups of coffee. The man looks up.

"No, man, we didn't ask for no coffee," he says. The woman turns her face up and it is like the sun rising. She is radiant in her sadness, thin to the point of being ethereal, translucent skin pulled tight over her bones with huge sad eyes and flame-red hair. A creature of almost pure spirit. I wonder if she is an angel, too.

"It's a gift." I push the cups towards her, but the man brushes them away.

"We don't need no gifts, man." He turns back to the woman and ignores me.

"Dulce, you gotta go back into rehab," he says. "Dulce, it's the only way to fight this thing and get better. You gotta go back and stop doing this to yourself before it kills you or you wind up in jail."

"Let me go, DB," she says.

Dulce looks up and sees that I am staring at her. There are small black dots and scars along the inside of her arms. She folds them over her chest, cradles a balled up pink sweater, looks up at me and tries to smile. She looks like one of the statues of the Madonna holding her child. At that moment, I am so sure that she's an angel that I start to tell her about myself.

DB turns to me and looks worried.

"You ain't just a clerk, are you?" he says.

I've smiled too big and he's seen who I am. I tone it down, but I can't lie.

"No."

He jumps between Dulce and me. "You can't arrest her. You can't just stand there and eavesdrop on people without a warrant or nothing, man. You got to tell us if you're a cop."

"I'm not a cop."

"I don't believe you. Run, Dulce, run. I'll hold him off." He's got his fists up now. "They can put *me* in jail."

Dulce hasn't moved or showed any reaction.

"Really, I'm not a cop. And I wouldn't arrest you if I were."

"Show me your card."

"What card? I'm not a cop."

"If you're a cop, you've got to show me your ID card. If you're not a cop, I figure you must have a card saying you're not a cop."

I think about that. It doesn't quite make sense, but who knows? I take out my wallet and turn so we can flip through it together. He looks at my ID.

"Donald? Never knew a cop named Donald. But who knows? Show me your credit cards, man."

I thumb the card section and there's nothing there.

"Nothing?" He looks at me like I'm an alien. "Never met nobody with nothing."

I shrug.

He studies my face, then pushes my wallet back to me.

"No Costco card, man. Every cop I know got a Costco card. Must buy bullets by the crate, get them from little old ladies handing out samples. You're still something, though. Convenience store zombies don't give away coffee." He turns back to the woman.

"But Dulce." He looks up at me but talks to her. He's wary now. "I mean, you've gotta go back. Back to the uh," he stares at me and searches for the word, "the castle. Yeah, the castle."

I smile and he seems relieved. He probably senses that I am an angel and can be trusted with secrets.

"Yeah," he says. "Go back to the castle. All the—uh—knights are there to help you. They'll give you everything you need so you can fight this thing. You can rule again, Dulce." He seems to hear his own words and then there are tears in his eyes as he repeats them. "You can rule, Dulce."

I see now that Dulce is not an angel but a delicate queen, probably fled from her kingdom (queendom?) to walk among ordinary folks for a time, just like I'm here for a time. Clearly, convenience store coffee is not good enough for royalty. I take the cups inside, pour them out and watch the princess and the servant who's been sent to return her to her kingdom far away. I try to imagine what they are saying. DB sees me watching them. He gathers her up and they walk away, his arm around her, protecting his sovereign.

I yell after her, "Rule the queendom!"

I won't tell you what DB yells back.

day two: 10:00 a.m.

knaves

About ten o'clock, I'm standing at the counter wondering if Dulce is my mission when my real mission walks in. I look up when I hear the little bell at the door and laugh when I see a man hurrying in with his head down, wearing a black ski mask on this hot day. I start to make a joke about the mask, but he pulls a gun out of his pocket and I just say, "Oh."

"Money," he says.

I smile now, as big as I can, and wait for the beatific glow to fill the room and turn his heart. No glow. I try harder and twist my face as hard as I can.

"Cut it out," he says.

I open my hand and extend it to him palm up in a gesture of peace.

"This is not the path God has laid out for you, my son," I say, sure that he can see the purity and righteousness of my appeal.

He slaps my hand away with the barrel of the gun.

"Please," I say, and smile some more. "Don't do this to yourself. One bad choice here can lead to years of wandering in darkness, until you repent and find your way back to the light." I smile bigger and try to show him the light, my smile against his gun.

The gun wins. He cocks it and shoves it into my face. He reaches over the counter past me, punches the button on the register and scoops out the cash.

As he runs out, I say, "I'm here when you're ready to come back to the light," to his back, but he doesn't slow down. The bell rings as he goes out the door. Maybe somewhere an angel just got their wings, but not here.

I call the police and it takes a little over an hour before they get here. I watch the windows and expect to see black and white cars skid into the parking lot with sirens blaring, maybe followed by a SWAT team, maybe led by the hot woman from the TV. Instead, one tired old woman shows up in a battered Ford.

"I'm Harriette," she says after she shows me her badge. I try to look to see if she has a Costco card behind it, but I can't tell.

"Just Harriette?" I say. "Not 'Detective Bosch' or 'Inspector Morse?' This is not like the TV shows."

"New policy. First names are friendlier." She doesn't smile. She looks like she has never smiled or slept. "Or so the policy says."

"Where is the rest of your team? CSI techs? Assistant district attorneys who solve crimes?"

She gives a little un-smile, probably the closest thing to an expression she's got. "Must be at the Huntsville Police Department's softball game." She opens a notebook, clicks a ballpoint pen and starts to write. When we're done, she looks up at me.

"So you were robbed of an indeterminate amount of cash by a man of average height wearing a black ski mask and black sweater?"

I nod vigorously, pleased that I've given her all the information she needs.

"It's important you catch him soon. He needs to begin his redemption so I can go home."

Harriette gives me a long, tired look. "We'll do what we can, sir."

"And just what is that, Detective? Will you pick him up today?"

She looks at me a long time and I'm afraid she's fallen asleep. I don't want to wake the poor old lady.

Finally, she says, "Probably not." She sighs. "Mostly, we knock on doors, sir. Knock on doors and file reports and knock on more doors. Every day there's more reports. Every day we knock on more doors. I'll work a double shift tonight—just like last night and the night before—knock on as many doors as I can around the neighborhood, see what I can come up with. It's how we solve crimes. Sometimes."

She starts to walk out and then turns around. "Oh, new department policy says I'm supposed to tell you to be optimistic about our chances of catching this guy."

"What are the chances?"

"Snowball in hell."

She leaves and the bell tinkles behind her.

day two: 3:00 p.m.

police work

I'm excited when Sancha comes in and I tell her about the robbery and the cops.

Her eyes are glowing. "So this guy just comes in, tough like, shoves the gun in your face and says, 'Gimme all your cash'?"

I nod.

"And you just open the register, cool like, and hand him the cash?"

"Something like that."

"Man. Wish I'd been here for that. Hope he comes back."

I feel bad that she missed it. For a minute I think about getting a gun and a ski mask and coming back to rob her, but though Sancha is small she is tough, and that might end badly. And I don't know where to get those things. Maybe Costco.

"The police are going to catch him tomorrow," I say. "Maybe they'll bring him in here and you can see him. If they bring him in and I'm not here, call me. He and I have something to work out. Do you think they'll let him serve his probation in the store, kind of like a halfway house with us putting his feet back on the path to righteousness?"

Sancha gives me a look like you give a cat that wants to go outside in a snowstorm.

"Man, the cops won't catch him. Cops never catch nobody."

"They do on TV. They catch them all."

"No, not even there. Think about it: cops just stumble around; somebody else has to actually solve the crime. Maybe a scientist, or a little old ladies' knitting club, or a man in a cape. Cops can't do nothing without some kind of angel doing the heavy lifting."

"You're right," I say, glad that Sancha has reminded me that this crime, this one lost soul, is my true mission and my path back to heaven. I look around to make sure I'm not glowing. "We are called to greatness in this mission."

"Who's this we? 'Called?' Are you back to talking like an old man, but a nicer one now? Or maybe somebody acting out a part in a medieval play? You're twenty-two, man. Act like it."

I start to explain to her that angels are timeless, but give up. Sancha looks away from me and back at the stack of books she doesn't want to study. "Yeah, us." She brightens. "Much more fun. Don and Sancha of the Q on a noble quest. Yeah, man, let's do it." She thinks a minute. "What'd he look like?"

"Oh, average height, black sweater."

"No, man, the picture."

I think a minute, then I give Sancha the cat look. "I don't think thieves hand out their picture."

"No, man, from the video system." She waits and she can see that I don't understand.

"C'mon." We go back into the storeroom. Sancha climbs up on the step ladder and hands me down rolls of toilet paper from the top shelf. When my arms are full of toilet paper, she comes to a black box with a little TV screen on it.

"I did not know this was here," I say.

"We don't brag about it because it's so cheap. Runs twenty-four hours on a VCR loop. I'm supposed to alternate the tape every day, but I never do."

She punches buttons and a black-and-white image of the empty counter comes up on the little screen. Sancha runs it in reverse and we see Harriette and me talking backwards and then me pacing around backwards. Finally, we come to the robbery. Sancha plays it a couple of times. She's excited when she pauses it at a frame that has the robber looking up at the camera.

She jumps down and runs back into the store. Did not know that Sancha's cool black hipster vibe let her run anywhere. She comes back with a laptop computer from her book bag and plugs a cable into the recorder. After a couple of minutes, she says, "There," and turns the laptop toward me with a big grin. She's got a picture of our robber staring out from her laptop. She unplugs the cable and hands her laptop down to me. She pops the ancient videotape out of the box and throws that down to me.

"Cops'll want this."

We go back to the counter and Sancha goes to work on her computer. Soon, we have a poster that says, "Have you seen this man?" in big black letters at the top over the picture of the robber. Below are the words, CALL HARRIETTE, with the police department's number.

"You gotta cover the counter for me," she says and snaps the laptop shut. "I gotta go to the library and print us some flyers."

She starts to walk out and I say, "How are you going to pay for them?"

She says thanks, walks back and grabs the three dollars and change that have come in since the register was last emptied an hour ago. The register does not complain and seems to be getting used to being empty. She comes back an hour later, and we leave the counter empty while we go around the neighborhood and put up flyers everywhere we can. It feels like Christmas, walking around the neighborhood handing out flyers to random strangers and seeing the look of surprise on their faces. I'm enjoying this mission more and more.

day two: 6:00 p.m.

they tell me i've got a husband and dogs

Harriette has one of the flyers in her hand when she comes in that afternoon. She puts the poster on the counter and says, "Didn't tell me you had video."

"Isn't it wonderful?" I shove the tape at her. "Now we just have to wait for someone to call."

She looks at the picture of the man in the black sweater and black ski mask a long, long time.

"Yeah, that'll work." She picks up the videotape. "Hope so. Spent the afternoon asking around about this robbery. I'll hit it again tomorrow morning early, before people go to work." She looks away. "But that's about all I can give this. There was a bank robbery last night. They pull all of us off these little cases when somebody hits a business with money and political juice. Sorry."

My face falls and I can see that she sees it.

"You cannot just give up," I say. "Is it not your mission to protect and serve everyone, not just the rich and mighty? How can you walk away from your God-given mission like this?"

Her mouth tightens into a straight line. "Policy says they're done paying me for overtime. Lieuten-ant says I'm on the bank job starting at five o'clock today."

"Well, I guess Sancha's right. We can't expect you police to solve crimes if we don't show you how. I'm just glad I've been put here to do the job. You go back to your policy."

She straightens up and her face darkens. She points her finger at me and starts to say something but then closes her mouth and drops her finger.

"Yeah," she finally says. "Maybe." She sighs. "After I'm done with the unpaid overtime on the bank job tonight, I'll knock on a few more doors for this, also unpaid." She pauses again. "Was kind of looking forward to having a night at home for once. They tell me I've got a husband and a couple of dogs there, but I'm not sure anymore."

She walks out and the bell tinkles behind her.

day two: 8:00 p.m.

good to have a plan

I had sent Sancha out for a rare dinner break and she gets back about eight. She almost trips over Dulce and DB, huddled outside again, but ignores them.

"How we doing, partner? Any word from Harriette?" Sancha's smiling. I didn't know she knew how. I tell her about Harriette being pulled off for the bank robbery and she loses the smile.

"Man, I told you, police can't do nothing no more except shoot us black folks. We got to solve this ourselves, not wait for help." She starts pacing.

"Have you presented yourself to our royalty?" I say with a little bit of a self-satisfied smile. She hasn't heard about our queen, and I get to tell her.

She looks at me and I point out the door.

"You mean the junkie out there?" she says. "Her brother trying his best to get her to go back to rehab? Yeah, man, tears your heart out just to listen to them."

"No," I smile at her earthly naiveté. "She's royalty. He's trying to get her to come home and take her rightful place on the throne, but her heart is so full of love she just wants to stay here among the common people."

Sancha looks at me. "She was talking about how strung out she was when I went by. Told DB her connection had a fresh supply and she had to get something tonight."

"No, my dear Sancha. Do you not see? She is a queen, probably talking to DB about a trade deal to lift her people up."

Then the truth hits me.

"I am such an idiot."

Sancha nods at me sadly. "No, man. Not an idiot. Just kind of . . . dreamy these days."

"How could I have missed it?" I pause and my eyes grow wide while Sancha waits for me. "I think perhaps you are right. Maybe there are drugs involved. But it's got to be DB that's the one on drugs. Maybe she has stepped down from the throne to come here to save her brother."

Sancha gives me that sad look again, but then she's excited, too. She grabs my arms. "That's it," she says. She's jumping up and down and I'm jumping up and down with her and we're happy and excited and jumping up and down together in the middle of the dark store.

"She is a queen," I say, thrilled that Sancha finally gets it.

"No. No, man, she's a junkie." She stops jumping. "Dulce's connection ran low on cash and he robbed us to get money to buy more. Now he's got product. We can follow Dulce tonight and she will lead us to her connection, and we'll get him."

Still jumping, I say, "You mean DB's connection?"

Sancha turns loose of my arms and looks at me again.

"Yeah, that's it," she says, but her mind is off planning now.

day two: 10:00 p.m.

clothes make the man (and woman)

Night-guy Atlas comes in early because Sancha said she'd give him some of her hours and the guy needs money. But when Sancha tells him what we're doing, Atlas brightens up from his perennial stupor.

"Catch a baddie," he says.

"Couldn't do it without you to cover things here, bud," says Sancha. She paws through a rack of hooded sweatshirts that stands by the counter, even though nobody in their right mind will buy a sweatshirt in Alabama in May. Sancha finds two black hoodies with the Quick Stop logo of a "Q" stylized into a flaming orange conquistador and throws one at me.

"We borrow these, blend in with the night so Dulce and DB can't see us following them. Bring the hoodies back when we're done."

We pull them on and admire ourselves. Sancha looks over and Atlas is giving her a puppy look. Sancha throws Atlas a matching sweatshirt. He pulls it on and stands up straight and proud.

Dulce and DB come in about two-thirty a.m. DB gets an energy drink and Dulce gets cigarettes. I notice that DB looks tired and nervous. Probably strung out and desperate.

I go up to Dulce and point at the cigarettes.

"You know those things will shorten your life? Probably be a real disappointment to all of the people whose lives you touch."

She laughs. "Yeah, all of them." She looks at me hard and her eyes go inside herself. I feel like I can read her mind and see her counting all the people who need her. When she gets to a high enough number, her eyes tear up.

I bow. DB gives me a funny look as they walk out the door. I look at Sancha for direction, but she is chanting something.

"One Mississippi, two Mississippi, three Mississippi."

"What's that mean?"

She glares and keeps on. "Four Mississippi, five Mississippi."

I grab her arm and tug. "They are getting away. You can do your meditation later."

"Three Mississippi—oh." Another glare. "Now you've messed me up. I wanted to give them a ten-second lead so they wouldn't see us. C'mon." She flips her hood up, I flip mine up and we're out the door. Dulce and DB are at the corner waiting for the light to let them cross Triana.

Sancha touches my arm. "Hang back here. See, when they cross, I'll follow them. You stay back.

After a minute or so, you catch up to me and I'll drop back. That way, if they look back, they'll see one person instead of two, and a different one each time, and they won't think we're following them."

"Yeah."

The first time I catch up to Sancha, she grabs my arm and pulls me back.

"Try to get close enough to hear what they say. Let me know what you find out. That's called 'gathering intelligence.'"

"Yeah, we need that."

Ahead, Dulce and DB stop and stare back at us. Sancha walks away. They start up again and I creep up behind them, an almost invisible black figure trailing them in the night.

The second time Sancha and I switch, DB takes Dulce's arm and they walk faster. Sancha and I stay with them. We hurry now, changing out every few seconds to stay close. At the Newson Road light, DB stops even though the light is green, and I almost run over them.

DB waits until the light turns red and the traffic starts to flow past us. He grabs Dulce's arm and they run across all four lanes, horns honking and brakes squealing, while we hesitate. By the time we know what's going on, they are across and the traffic is full speed. When we finally get across, they've disappeared into the neighborhood.

day three: 4:00 a.m.

duct tape solves everything

"Oh man," says Sancha. We wander, muttering, through the neighborhood hoping to find them. We eventually come back to Triana somewhere between my house and the store.

"What now?" I ask Sancha.

"Don't know, man. Just go back to the store, put the sweatshirts up, go home. Stupid idea, man. Don't know why I ever thought we could do this."

I want to tell her that I am an angel and we can do anything, but that seems silly and hollow and meaningless. Whoever sent me down here had a lot more confidence than I have in myself right now.

We walk along without looking up much. We pass the storefront church and a voice says, "God needs you, brother. And sister."

Sancha turns away. "God made a mistake."

The voice laughs harshly. "Damned straight."

We walk on a couple more houses before Sancha stops and says, "That ain't the preacher."

"Well, of course it was. Who else would station themselves at a church in the middle of the night?"

"Look again."

I look back at a different man than I saw yester-day. "You're right."

Sancha says, "The real preacher does a lot of good for folks, takes care of people that don't have homes or jobs or food. That guy there's running some kind of scam."

She stares for a long time.

"That's our guy," she says. She walks back fast and I have to run to catch up to her.

"How can you possibly know that?"

"It's a guess, but we got to take a chance. Stick with me and play along."

The guy who is not the preacher smiles when we walk up, big smile on his mouth but not in his eyes.

"God wants you," he says, flat, like it's just something to say.

"And we want God," Sancha has the same flat look.

"Thought so." The guy's smile is all big now. He opens the door to the church.

"Good setup here," says Sancha.

The guy laughs. "Preacher man leaves the place unlocked at night to help out people in the neighborhood with no place to go. I figure I'm helping out the neighborhood, too, giving people what they need. I stand in the doorway and say,

'God wants you.' Anybody looking to buy knows to tell me they're looking for God."

"Yeah, that's what I guessed," says Sancha.

"Guessed? Who told you about me, anyway?" He acts like it's a casual question, but he blocks the doorway with one hand behind his back until Sancha answers.

"Dulce."

The guy laughs again. I don't like his laugh. "You just missed her. She ought to be real happy by now."

He leads us inside, just behind the picture window. The room is half-painted, the room piled with drop cloths and rollers and boxes of supplies. He opens a cardboard box off to one side.

"Pick your poison," he says.

"It's for him," Sancha motions at me.

"It most certainly is not," I say, but I look at Sancha glaring at me and I change my story. "At least not most of the time. I just need a little bit of help right now."

There's that laugh again that I hate so much. I bend over the box and look inside at neat rows of plastic baggies holding white powders and green herbs. I start to reach in and the guy slaps my hand.

"Cash first," he says.

I hesitate and his eyes narrow. "I don't know you." He reaches behind his back and his hand comes out with a silver gun glittering in the darkness.

I throw my head back and stretch my arms out like wings. "I am proud to die for my mission."

He's confused. In the moment of his confusion, Sancha jumps in from the side, higher than I would have imagined her capable of, with her arms over her head like she's flying. But the gun comes around faster than she is moving and I think the gun is going to win, but then a blinding light from heaven flashes in the window and they both look out the window and freeze.

Except that gravity doesn't freeze. Sancha crashes onto him. The car that lit us all up turns away, and I'm left blinking in the semi-darkness trying to sort out the groans and shapes on the floor. Sancha is yelling, "Duct tape! Duct tape!" and I think it's a bad joke from the home improvement show on TV until I realize what she wants.

I pick up a roll of duct tape and wrap it around and around the guy until the tape runs out. The guy squirms and curses.

Sancha grins.

"Got him," she says, and laughs. I like this laugh.

"We must be sure it is the robber," I say. I turn to the guy. "Do you own a handgun?"

Sancha picks up the gun from the floor. She holds it up to me.

"Well," I say. "Do you own a black ski mask?"

He still hasn't answered when we get him up on his feet and march him and his box and his gun out of the church and down the street to the

Q. We call the police station and they tell us they will send Harriette out as soon as they can.

day three: 5:00 a.m.

for the kingdom

Harriette comes in at five, a couple of hours before her usual starting time. Her face falls when she sees a man taped up at the counter. She looks back at the bright smiles on Sancha's face and mine. She looks back at the fake preacher. He looks back at us.

"When you called and said you had something," she says, "I thought you meant you had an address or something. Wanted to talk to you before you did anything stupid." She pauses. "Like this."

"No," I say. "We've got the robber, got his box of drugs, and got his gun." I wave the gun in the air. Harriette steps up and takes it from me.

Sancha tells her the story. Harriette sighs, and I am so proud. I hope I will not be taken back to heaven before we get the robber into jail and that I can work with him on his redemption.

"Well," says Harriette. She seems less excited than I expected, but Harriette is not exactly an excitable girl.

"Well," she says again. "Good to get this guy off the street. I guess. Maybe for a day." She looks away from us. "Can't imagine a judge will have any trouble with this search."

Sancha nods her head, but she's smiling less.

"Well," Harriette says again, "Let me take him in and see what we can do. I think I'm going to leave you two out of this. Hey! We had a crazy report from a drunk citizen last night, something about seeing two superheroes in black costumes flying around a church. Maybe I'll say they left this mook there. Give everybody a good story."

"So we don't get a reward?"

Harriette just looks at me. She gets the guy to his feet.

"At least you've got him on the robbery," I say.

Harriette shakes her head. "This isn't your robber. I was coming by to tell you. We got the robber—the real one—last night about two in the morning. I knocked on the door of a guy who answered in his underwear with a crack pipe in his hand. He gave up his buddy for the robbery rather than take the drug bust. We picked up the robber, he confessed to the robbery here, now he's trying to give us somebody bigger to stay out of jail himself. Way it usually goes, out in the real world."

At the door, with one hand on the robber and Sancha holding the door, Harriette turned back to me and gives me the closest thing to a smile that she has.

"We wouldn't have got the robber if you hadn't pushed me, though. Thanks." She pauses and points her chin at the fake preacher. "And thanks for this. But please don't ever do it again." She laughs, or I think it is a laugh. "Leave that to the superheroes."

The bell rings as they leave and I feel behind my back. No wings.

Sancha and I follow Harriette out and watch her load the fake preacher and the drugs into her car and drive off. Dulce and DB are on the sidewalk, silent until Harriette drives away. As soon as she leaves, DB starts begging Dulce, but she keeps shaking her head. Finally, she gets up and starts to stumble away from him. DB starts to cry.

He stands up and yells at her back, sobbing and screaming with a face full of pain and tears, "Dulce, you gotta do the hard work even when you don't know what you're doing. That's the only miracle we've got down here. You've got to try rehab again, on faith. Please." Dulce turns around and stands there with a sad look. Then she looks at me.

"Maybe," she says. "One more time." She sees me and the tiniest hint of a smile blooms uncontrolled on her sad face, like a child peeking around the corner on Christmas morning. "For the kingdom. Tomorrow."

I walk in to Sancha. "I'm not sure that I completely understand what's going on with their magical language. But it is beautiful."

"Yeah. I'm not sure what you understand either, man. But maybe it will be beautiful."

Sancha goes home. The bell rings behind her and I smile. I take Dulce and DB some coffee. DB eyes my outstretched hand like it's a snake, then reaches out and takes the cup.

"Thanks," he says.

I nod. "It's why I'm here."

Maybe.

day three: 8:30 a.m.

lose something?

Across town from the Q, two young women climb into a rental car at the Huntsville International Airport. The tall one snaps her seat belt. "Seems like a quiet, peaceful, all-American town."

The short one in the driver's seat adjusts the car's mirrors. Precisely. "Don't get ahead of yourself. We're still at the airport. It's just an airport."

Tall says, "Be specific: We're at the Huntsville Airport for the first time. Use your FBI training in deduction. No trash in the parking lot. No homeless. All-American."

Short pushes back. "Use your bureau skepticism. Collect facts. Like the fact that we're still seven miles from our target."

"Six-point-nine. We've got to be precise, if we want to lose our nicknames."

Short sighs. "We must be earning some respect back. They wouldn't have put us in charge of finding an item like this if they still thought of us as Cheech and Chong."

"We can't be too careful." She studies the short one's clothes. "Acceptable outfit. Professional pant suit. Dark gray."

"You too. Nothing frivolous there. All black and white."

Tall says, "For next time, though, I would suggest that your lavender blouse might remind someone that, while we are FBI, we are not FBI men."

Short grinds her teeth. No point in fighting with what the bureau has made clear is her last-chance partner, and not much of a partner at that. She looks for something agreeable to say.

"You're right about Huntsville. Why would someone want to blow it up?"

"Don't know. But a stolen nuclear device will accomplish that purpose."

"True that."

Tall says, "Watch the slang."

The short one puts the black, nondescript, late-model, made-in-America rental sedan in gear and heads toward the FBI Terrorist Explosive Device Analytical Center (TEDAC) *day three: 3:30 p.m.*

things that belong in an envelope

I go home at the end of a very successful day, and—Oh My God!—my good fortune continues.

There is mail in my mailbox. I hope it's for me.

Three letters. I take them inside and spread them out on the kitchen table.

The first letter has a splashy picture and my name and address, which I already know. It is from the Chevrolet dealership. I start to open the envelope and realize that this is not how I open letters. I go to the bedroom, retrieve the letter opener from my desk, and carefully and properly open the envelope with a smooth cut at the spine. I'm excited. Maybe I own a Chevy! There's not one parked here, or at the Q, but maybe they have one waiting for me at the dealer.

They do! If I bring them money, my car is wait-ing for me. The price is unclear, but it is thousands of dollars less now than it was last week, and they will give it to me for less than they would charge their own grandmother.

As excited as I am about getting a car, I decide that an angel can't take a car from a grandmother, and reluctantly set that letter aside.

The next envelope is as big as both of my hands. I turn it over and read giant red words warning me I have to act now, or I am in danger of losing my Medicare. Panicked, I open the envelope and find helpful information on when and how I must sign up. But it's based on my birthday so I'm going to have to check on that. My palms are sweating as I open my wallet to see if I'm too late. I still have just a driver's license and thirty-seven dollars in cash. No credit cards, no pictures, and—perhaps importantly—no Medicare card. I look at the birth-date on the license, back to the flyer, and mentally calculate that—at the age of twenty-two—I have 15,453 days to sign up.

I decide not to act now. Perhaps I'll file this away for later. If I have a filing cabinet.

The third letter has an angry man shaking a fist and demanding that I join him to protect my Medicare. I counsel him to relax, and put that letter, unopened, on top of the other valuable packets.

Then I decide to throw them all out. I scoop them up and carry them to the kitchen trash can, and step on the pedal that opens the shiny can. The lid pops open. Just as I release my mail into the can's jaws, I see a piece of paper in the bottom. I retrieve today's mail and fish out the paper.

It is a plain white envelope, with my name and address handwritten in blue ink. I look at it and see that it has been ripped open. That seems unnecessarily violent. I look in the envelope and find that there is nothing there.

I turn the envelope back over and study the writing. No postmark, or stamp. It's been two days since my awakening—that's what I'm calling it today. Was this before or after that? Yesterday, I thought that meant I was an angel. Today, I don't know. Do angels get mail?

It's the return address I stare at. 504 Greendale, in my hometown of Huntsville, Alabama. I look at it and I'm filled with an overwhelming sadness.

I read the address piece-by-piece, and try to break it down and find what makes me sad. No sadness in Huntsville. It's a mid-sized Southern city, famous for building moon rockets, and once, raising cotton. Home for me. I'm not sure if I've ever lived anywhere else. And, like most places you've always been, it feels neither good nor bad.

This 504 Greendale has no meaning to me. I can't tell you where it is or what it is. But it seems like a very sad place. The energy drains out of me and I collapse into my living room's one chair and try to pull meaning out of the tiny footprint of ink.

It won't come. I reach for the remote and turn on the TV. I watch three murders and decide that these murders don't teach me anything more about this world than the seventeen murders I watched two nights ago. Turning off the TV, I walk around my small house twice looking for a clue. Four square rooms with a tiny bathroom tucked between the two bedrooms. I walk around and find nothing. I sleep a few hours, but the answers aren't in my dreams.

When I wake up I get ready to go back to the Quick Stop. But with my hand on the door, I realize I'm missing something. I pick up a neatly-folded cloth from the side of the kitchen sink and wipe everything down.

Everything, including the water bottle inside the refrigerator and the doorknob on the way out. Feels like something I'm supposed to do.

day three: 6:00 p.m.

nobody's home

After Sancha finishes her shift, we walk out in search of the address. We're sitting on a curb in a parking lot on Drake Avenue close to the Parkway, maybe a half mile from the Q, taking a break.

"We're going to have to get a car," says Sancha, "if we're going to start running all over town chasing your past."

I point across the street. "There used to be an A&W Root Beer there, with a fireplace and root beer floats."

"Car lot now. What's wrong with your head? Know a lot of useless old stuff, but can't remember what you had for breakfast two days ago?"

"Don't other people's brains work like this?"

She snorts, stands up and brushes the grit off of her jeans. "Walking is taking longer than I planned. When I looked it up, I thought 504 Greendale was just around the corner."

I stand up and brush myself off like she did. "We are fortunate that you put a sign on the Q telling our customers that we were closed. Be courteous to anyone who might come by."

She snorts again. "Yeah. Maybe convince them not to come back."

"Is that why you wrote, CLOSED FOR REMODEL-ING?"

"C'mon. Screw 'em if they can't take a joke. Besides, we get like two customers a day. Nobody's coming. Except maybe your junkie friend."

"Maybe the owner will drop in. Maybe we'll get fired."

She stares at me and bursts into laughter. I laugh with her even though I don't know why that's funny.

"Even the old guy that worked there before me, back when they sold beer and cigarettes, said he'd never seen the owner. All the owner knows is the bank deposits. Maybe not even that."

She turns and I follow. We cross the Parkway, a very busy road. Drivers give us a wave with just one finger and I cheerfully return a full wave back.

We come to 504 Greendale. The grass hasn't been cut and there's not a car in the driveway.

"Maybe nobody's home." I pull back.

"Maybe they are," she says.

I turn away. "This was a stupid idea. What are you proposing we do? Knock on the door and say, do you know me? This is pointless."

"What? You scared now?"

"No." I look at the house. "Just . . . sad at the wasted time."

"Well, put your feelings aside. They ain't going to help you now."

She walks up to the door, rings the bell and then knocks. I hang back, but then join her on the con-crete stoop.

"Look at this." She points at the three deadbolts on the door. "Guy's paranoid. We ain't going to get in here if nobody's home."

Something occurs to me. "The back door is open."

"Fort Knox on the front, Grand Central Station in the back? C'mon. Why you think you know that?"

I don't budge. She jumps off the stoop, grumbling, and we go around the back. There is a small concrete patio with a green door. The door has three locks, too, but the wood is splintered and hangs away from the frame. She pushes and the door swings open.

"Hello," she calls. Nobody answers. She repeats that a couple of times and gestures me to go in.

"No."

"We're just going to look around. We'll call out every few feet in case someone's there."

"No."

"Well I'm not coming all this way without a peek." She disappears into the door.

I step back. The door looks like the yawning black mouth of a monster in a movie. I'm wondering what I'm going to tell Harriette if Sancha doesn't come out.

No need. There's a shadow at the door and Sancha steps out.

"Nothing there, man. No furniture, not a scrap of paper, not even a mouse turd. Nothing."

day three: 8:00 p.m.

kick up a little dust

"Sorry the house was a dead end." Sancha puts the rusty key in the lock and opens the door to the Quick Stop. She throws the Closed for Remodeling sign on the sidewalk with the other trash.

I have to be careful to step around DB and Dulce. "Maybe. Maybe we never know where the road goes when we start it."

"Deep, Confucius. Put it in a fortune cookie. I'm going to explore the path of napping behind the counter."

I pick up Sancha's sign and turn it back and forth like an oracle. Finally, I crease it horizontally, fold it in half and balance it on a ledge at the window so that only the word "remodeling" shows.

Sancha squints one lazy eye open and peeks out at me from where her head rests on her folded arms on the counter. "What's that for?"

"The sign said we were closed for remodeling. We're not closed now. We never close." I realize that we just opened. "Except when we do. But we're not closed now."

"Then leave it on the floor where I put it."

"But we're not just open, either. We need a sign to tell people we are remodeling."

"We're not remodeling; it was a joke while we snuck out. Owner won't even pay for lights or toilet paper for the bathrooms."

"We told the world we were remodeling. We must remodel."

"People say a lot of things, Don, and don't really mean them. Get used to it."

I think about it. "That's not the way it should be. You tell people you're remodeling, you ought to remodel." I take the broom away from the wall and lean on it. "Anyway, it's something to do until my mission comes along." I sweep a pile of dead rats, gum wrappers and an old church flyer out the door.

"Hey!" says DB as the cloud sails past.

He stands up and reads the sign. "We can help. I could use some work. Dulce, too."

Another thing to figure out. I scratch my head and think. "Work is a good thing. Help is, too. But we can't pay anything." I look around and do a sad inventory of what we've got to offer. "Well, except for coffee, and expired peanut butter crackers and fountain drinks if you use an old cup."

"Better than sitting on the sidewalk bitching. And any calories we can get into Dulce is better than she had yesterday."

I pass the broom to DB. Dulce uncoils herself and stands with the slow grace that only the truly noble have. I pick up a roll of paper towels and a spray bottle of cheap cleaner and guide her to the windows.

Sancha is watching this from behind the counter, probably wishing she had stayed asleep. After five minutes of watching Dulce shove the same dirt around the same place on the glass, and occasionally taking a small sip from the Mountain Dew in the faded cup at her elbow, Sancha mutters a curse, picks up a rag and goes to dusting.

The Q brightens like someone's turned up the lights. Dulce has rubbed one small porthole in the grime and the setting sun pours in. The light dances across the floor and flows into me and blooms into a smile. Even a fragile queen can serve. I whistle a tune, but don't know where it comes from.

day three: midnight

big bad bomb

In the back corner of the Threat Command Center in the basement of the FBI's TEDAC in the middle of Redstone Arsenal outside of Huntsville, the women they call Cheech and Chong are sharing a folding table. They have to duck their heads under the seal with the FBI's new motto, "The FBI Protects Good Americans." While the motto is part of the government's new push for more aggressively folksy clarity, the Threat Command Center has added their own slogan underneath the FBI slogan: "Don't Blow Nobody Up." Hopefully, at least one of them will prove to be true.

"Midnight," says the short Hispanic woman they call Cheech.

Chong unfolds herself from the laptop she has been typing on. The table is too small for her tall frame. She is stiff, sore, and cranky.

"Two hours in coach on a plane, almost ten hours in these metal chairs." She pops her back. "Interrupted by ten seconds at the command lectern at the front of the room."

Cheech puts her head down on the table and the table rocks. "Please let me forget that."

"No. Hold onto that. We're going to be back up there someday. Didn't it feel good to march into a room full of bigwigs and senior agents, jump up on the stage and say, 'Ladies and Gentlemen, we are Agents Chavez and Zhong, and we have been sent here from headquarters to take charge of the effort to secure this missing device, and—with your help—that is what we are going to do for this great country?'"

"Felt really, really good when the boss told us to get our asses over to the data entry table. Felt even better when he put his hand on his head and said, 'Leave my hair alone,' and everybody laughed."

"Answers the question of whether they all know about that."

They both think back to the time they ripped the wig off the head of the President and shot it, thinking it was a rabid squirrel. The FBI had graciously declined to release their names, so the press had dubbed the tall Zhong and the shorter Chavez with the nicknames "Cheech and Chong."

"Well, at least he knows who we are."

Zhong folds herself back to her work. Chavez raises her head and looks at the command podium and the wall of three large video screens.

The left screen is divided into halves. The top half has a rotating picture of what looks like a fantastically beautiful necklace made of beads that seem to change from emeralds to rubies to glowing stones unknown on this earth, with a shimmering peace symbol attached. At the top of the screen the label reads: MK-397 SUPER-MINIATURIZED AMERI-CAN BEAUTY PEACE-KEEPING DEVICE. Over the top of the picture, technical data scrolls with the bomb's serial number, its weight (0.347 pounds), and its MAS rating, which is the radius of Maximum Aw Shit damage, the name chosen in the new spirit of government clarity and folksiness.

The MAS of the device is 438.7 miles.

The bottom half shows an ordinary-looking silver hat box. It rotates and opens and closes while the text explains that the box is made of a secret lightweight material much denser than lead. The device must be kept tightly closed in the box to prevent radioactivity from escaping.

Chavez says, "Can't be real."

She turns back to the wall. The center holds a screen that is so large that it is only used for classified intelligence and college football games. It shows a map of the North American continent, centered on Huntsville. Every five seconds, the screen pings and a circle of flames grows outward from Huntsville to the MAS.

The screen on the right holds a large spreadsheet of all of the major players of the task force, with their role, location, and an instantaneous contact button.

Chavez studies the screen, makes a "mppph" sound and stands up. She goes over to the keyboard below the screen and adds the names

"Chavez" and "Zhong" at the bottom, with the role of INTEL and returns to her mission.

day three: midnight

trust your boss

The door behind the podium opens and a small man with an authoritative head of short, executive-style white hair and a steely-eyed gaze walks in. He ignores Zhong and Chavez and walks up to the ping screen. He studies the screen for several cycles, rocking back and forth enough that Zhong, who watches him without raising her head from her work, worries that he might fall.

He walks a crooked path over to them. "So they've left you girls in charge?"

Zhong says, "Yes, sir. Looks that way. Mr. Vice—"

"Just Bob. Or Mr. Pilgrim. I'm incognito, so please don't use my title. But this mission is so important that the President sent me here to take charge personally. Or to get me out of Washington again."

"Yes, sir. But may I ask you a question?"

"Of course, young lady. I'm here to help you grow. And to save the world."

"Yes, sir. But I wasn't going to ask about that." She points at the bomb board. "Sir, I have a master's degree in physics." Chavez rolls her eyes at the ass-kissing. "And I don't recall any element with either the explosive power of this device, or the radiation absorption properties of the container."

The man with the authoritative hair, who has a degree in business from a northeastern college famous for awarding impressive degrees to rich but dumb sons of politicians, says, "We are the United States government. We can invent any element we need."

"Yes, sir. But why a necklace?"

"The President wanted the First Lady to wear it as a sign of American power. Until it was pointed out to him that there were several problems with that plan. None convinced him until the scientist who built this pointed out—damned scientists are always negative—that the radiation would make the First Lady even more tanned than he is. By then, the device was already complete."

"But it's a one-of-a-kind?"

"It is now. The damned scientist who created it is the only one who knows how to create the elements, and he's disappeared. He also came up with the secret code that he said is the only way to save mankind from this device, if it's ever activated."

"What is it?"

"How would I know? It's in the manual somewhere."

He points at the ping screen. "And you still have no location?"

Up close, the smell of bourbon explains the rocking.

"No sir." Zhong knows she should leave it at that, but she knows she may not have many opportunities to impress. "But the instant the terrorists open the container shielding the device, the AN-45 Specific Radiation Detector will display the location on the board, and you and every agent in the field will be instantly alerted to begin recovery."

He studies her. She hopes it's admiration, but she's afraid he might be about to throw up.

"Excellent. You girls will make fine agents someday."

"Sir, we're already—"

"You girls got the data entered yet? You're holding up the team." He studies the board with the patriotic look he normally reserves for campaign billboards. "Two new people on the roster. Don't know who those boys are, but we can use every man we can get. Have to find something to put them to work on."

day three: midnight

find the heart of the sadness

There's a sadness here in my little home.

I've walked home dead tired, but proud of the start of remodeling the Q, a small mission I have taken on now that Harriette has assured me that our criminal justice system can be counted on to rehabilitate our robber and the drug dealer. Now—with hot sauce dripping down my chin and my belly full of happy taco fire, sure that my big mission is coming soon—I am as happy as the birds singing in the night. I remember grumpy, cynical Sancha singing an upbeat Lady Gaga tune, then Dulce—Dulce!—humming along as she smeared the windows. I smiled. It was a good day to be an angel on a small break from my main mission.

I whistle that same tune as I walk up to my door and put the key in. I cross the threshold and Lady G's song dies in my throat with a strangled gurgle. I try to pick it up again, and I can't remember the words. Or the tune.

But it is more than that. Like a stroke victim, it is there in my head, but I can't touch it. I step back outside, and the words flow out of me again. Step in, and the music is replaced by a vague, fearful sadness.

I try to get a handle on the feeling. My emotions are running away with me, simultaneously scream-ing at me, and refusing to talk to me and explain themselves.

I stand very still and let my body choose on its own. It sits down in my chair and turns on the TV.

Watching, I see the first murder. Only then do I feel at home.

Is this a part of my change, or is this what homes are like for everybody in this place and time? Do we all spend years and treasure to build homes to try to shelter ourselves, but in the end we do such a good job of following everyone else's rules for better homes that we wind up with places that strangle our unique selves, leaving us sad strangers within our own choices? Only comfort-able when we hide in a made-up world where all problems can be solved by the commercial break, rather than finding our own missions? Is this all I had in life, a vague slippery regret drowning out all the music, listening to a TV box sing of death because I've strangled my own songs? Is this all there is for people now?

Damned if I know. It feels like thinking leaves me feeling confused and alone.

I force myself to turn off the TV. I stand and put out my hands like I'm holding a divining rod. I leave the lights off, relying on the muted street lights from the windows. Try to do what comes natural and see where this feeling takes me.

I slowly spin around in the living room. No pictures on the walls. One chair, but it's soft. Decent TV. The man I was didn't need more than one chair. One butt, one chair, comes to me in a voice like a rule for living.

The bedroom seems the same: comfortable, but no extravagances.

The house of a man with other things on his mind.

Not a lot in the kitchen. The food is basic but bland: bread, peanut butter, oatmeal cookies. I recognize the brands from the Quick Stop. Hidden behind three cans of chicken noodle soup is one half-empty bottle of hot sauce, like a secret vice.

And, judging from the fact that the guy in the food truck gave me hot stuff without being asked, hot sauce is something I was eating before the Awakening. But I felt like I needed to wolf it down and finish it before I got home. A man who lives alone but feels that he has to keep secrets from someone there.

I retrace my steps around the house, letting the feelings wash over me and trying to name them. Bedroom feels like . . . anxiety. Like tossing and turning when you know you should sleep but there's something else you've got to do.

The chair feels comfortable. Not just to sit in, but to look at. Resigned, but comfortable. Kind of like a sigh. I wonder if everyone has one of these.

The kitchen feels like an empty belly.

I'm walking from the kitchen into the small hall when the full sadness crashes over me. There is a small half-door, down low in the hall next to the kitchen. The walls and ceiling are all white-painted here, and the door has that crinkly look of something that's been painted over many times.

Just a utility door, but I can feel the sadness grow and fade as I walk closer and then pull away. Sitting on the floor in front of it, the sadness becomes palpable, a spiritual nausea when I reach my hands out toward the door.

I think about it a long time before I put my hand on the plain white knob. When I touch it, an orange explosive heat flashes through me. I jerk my hand back and look at it, but it's not burned.

Something tells me that I can't sit here too long, but I don't want to go yet. I put my left hand over my right, grab the door and pull hard against the fire. The door won't open. Even when I brace against the wall and push with my feet, the door won't budge.

Enough. I stand up. I'm exhausted and going to bed.

As my eyes close, the thought wanders into my head, unbidden like most thoughts do. The door is something that should be open and is stuck. Maybe that's why it makes me sad.

Whatever the reason, there is a sadness here. At least for me.

day four: 6 a.m.

maybe, just for you

There is a fog at dawn as I walk up to the Q just to get out of the house and go somewhere that might house my destiny. And, this morning, I see a clear sign that this is the place. The Q, which had always squatted like a darkened shame next to the closed Laundromat that shares the building, is bathed in a heavenly glow.

All I have to do now is follow the light.

As I step into the parking lot, I'm baptized in glowing white water droplets from the early morning fog. I see that the light is not shining on the Q from above, but coming from inside. The Q is a shining jewel in a blanket of white clouds. I open the door and the bell tinkles.

Atlas is up on a stepladder with a long fluorescent light bulb in his hand. The ceiling here always looked like the dark mouth of a homeless man with a few scattered white teeth. Atlas pops the bulb into the last fixture, and now the Q has its own glowing sky illuminating the store and spilling out into the neighborhood.

"Wow," I say. "Atlas holds up the world with the power of his light."

He grins a crooked smile down at me and flexes his arms. He's a squat bodybuilder with a fondness for muscle shirts. Flexing and posing are the only ways I've ever seen him show thanks or approval, so I guess this is good.

"Owner paid for this?"

He shakes his head as he climbs down and hoists the ladder with one hand. "Next door."

These are the most words I've ever heard Atlas say, but I still don't understand.

"I still don't understand," I say.

He jerks his head at the wall and I try to translate that into words.

"The closed Laundromat next door?"

He nods and seems to think that explains everything.

"These came from next door?"

"Big pile in there." A little irritation at having to communicate the clearly obvious. "Be careful. You drop them, they explode. Watch this." He picks up a tube from the floor, rubs it furiously with the tail of his shirt, and the light glows in little flashes.

"Cool. How did you get in next door?"

He folds up the ladder and stomps to the stockroom with it, irritated at all this conversation, comes out empty-handed, goes behind the counter and pulls out the rusty key to the Q that we rarely use because the door's open twenty-four hours. He shakes it at me. I shrug, and he points at our door and the wall between us and the Laundromat.

"Our key fits both places?"

He rolls his eyes yes and snatches up his backpack. Walking out, he gives me an impatient look when he sees I'm still confused. He stops, looks at me, and sighs.

"Lot of old shit in there, Don."

Exhausted from the word-effort, he shoves the door open with his shoulder and flexes his arm to say he's going to the gym.

The Q looks so festive I decide I need to brighten up, too. I go to the T-shirt rack, and select a bright yellow Q shirt and pull it over my own shirt.

DB and Dulce have come inside, which I think is good. They're slumped on the floor by the drink fountain. Dulce is sipping on a Mountain Dew and shaking. I should have warned her about the caffeine. DB has a dirty newspaper, turning the pages.

"Lot going on," he says. "I haven't read a paper in years. Don't believe what's happened to my country."

I think about that, resolve to go to a library later and ask the librarian what's happened to America in the last few years. They live for questions like that.

Dulce says, "DB, I gotta have something more."

"Dulce, you can't. Try to make it to the end of the day. Maybe just lunch time, lie down then, take a nap, let it all go away for a little while."

Dulce looks up with her amazing dark blue eyes with forest green tinges around the outer edges. Through it all, the whites of her eyes are luminously clear and huge against the shrunken skin. I look at her eyes and think, I could never say no to eyes like that.

DB can't, either.

"Dulce, I shouldn't trade you stuff for a promise, after all the times you've had to break promises in the past. But this once. I've got a little left from the baggie we bought the other night. Just a little. Snort it, don't shoot up. I'll give you that right now if you promise you'll go with me to the rehab center after."

He looks at me and adds, "I mean the palace."

"Yeah, I promise."

Her voice is so listless that even I wonder if her words have meaning. I see DB's face go through a hundred contortions: anger, disappointment, and outrage from a thousand images from his past. I feel like I can see them, too, somehow invited into my mind without understanding what I see. But the look settles on the sadness of the here and now and his eyes grow moist as he reaches into the shopping bag at his side, and pulls out a plastic sandwich bag with a small pile of a fine-grained white powder. Dulce licks her lips. He pulls it back.

"Just a little."

She nods.

"And you promise?"

She nods her head, but it looks like it's something done by a puppet, with no connection to her.

The water is starting to overflow in DB's eyes.

"No, I mean it, Dulce. You promised yesterday, and the day before. You give me so many of these bullshit promises that they're not even worth the words anymore. But you're slipping so far away from me I don't know if I'm ever going to get you back. I got to have a real promise from you this time."

Another puppet head nod. DB pulls the packet back but we both know no man can resist the eyes of the queen. He starts to bring it forward, then he stops.

"No. Wait. We've clouded over so many words that promises to me don't mean nothing anymore between us. Promise Don."

She looks at me and I can feel my insides melting.

But something is happening to her, too, as she looks into my eyes. She starts to mutter the same old rote throwaway, but the words catch. She tries to look away but it's like all the light in the room focuses into a bright gossamer thread binding our visions together, and she can't.

Finally, she locks eyes with me. "I. Promise. You. Don."

I'm about to hug her, but DB offers her the packet and her attention runs away from me. She grabs the bag like a hungry animal, puts it up to her nose and inhales it. Turns the baggie inside out and licks it clean. Her face brightens as if all the blood that had been drained out of her is suddenly pumped back.

"Wow. That must be good stuff, DB," I say.

He looks at me with anger, then retreats behind a defensive wall. "Just sugar, man. You know how kids get sugar highs? She needs one sometime. That's all it is, man. Don't tell your cop buddy nothing different."

"Sure. Good to know it's just sugar."

I notice that the floor looks dirty again, even though I mopped it yesterday. I guess light changes things. I get the mop and bucket and give it one more go. As I finish, I see DB trying to help Dulce stand.

"C'mon. The . . . palace is right around the corner. You can make it."

She has more energy, but not much. He pulls her arm, but she slaps him away.

"Not you," she says. "Him."

day four: 9:00 a.m.

only the best

As DB is explaining to me where the palace is, two young women in black suits walk into the Q. The tall Asian woman comes in first but the short Hispanic woman hustles to get in the lead. She speaks while her companion looks over her head and sweeps the building as if she is memorizing every detail.

"Good morning, sirs."

Sancha says, "Good morning, officers."

"We're not officers."

Sancha says, "And I'm not a sir, ma'am."

Short cocks her head at Sancha and smiles.

The tall one corrects, "Well, we might be. Officers."

Short says, "Never can tell."

I say, "Whatever you are, how can we help you?"

"Coffee," says Short.

"Please," adds Tall.

Sancha leads our merry little band to the coffee machine, stepping over Dulce.

Short one looks down. "Might be the place."

Tall says, "I don't think it was the coffee that did that."

"Still, bodes well."

Sancha studies the short one as if trying to figure out what that means. Short catches her glance and they exchange a look that lingers a second longer than it needs to.

"Could we have a sample of the coffee?"

Sancha's not sure where this is going. "Sample?"

I say, "What a cool idea. Maybe we'll start having regular coffee tastings."

Sancha and Short say, "Yeah" at the same time but it doesn't feel like it's agreement. More like both of them showing the other how tough and cynical they can be.

I get two of the old cups from Dulce's stack and put a taste in each.

Short says, "Jesus."

Tall nods when she takes her taste. "That is remarkably bad."

Sancha says, "Can't arrest us for bad coffee."

"Arrest you? We need to thank you."

Sancha leans back in her tough street pose and crosses her arms, demanding an answer.

Short laughs, "See, we work for—"

Tall says, "—an unspecified government agency."

"Yeah. An unspecified government agency. So we are highly-trained professionals."

Sancha says, "Should be highly respected."

"Exactly. We're at—"

Tall says, "—an unspecified location."

"Preparing for an important meeting that will require our expertise, and the big boss tells us to go get coffee for everybody. He says it's an honor. We should be the best at selecting coffee because we're—"

Sancha says, "—chicks. Yeah, I get it. Happens everywhere. But what are you going to do; it's the way of the world."

Short shakes her head. "No. We're doing some-thing about it, and you're going to help us. We figure if we take 'em the worst coffee on earth, we'll be off the hook and—"

Sancha says, "Show 'em that just because you don't have balls doesn't mean you don't have balls."

Short admires her. "Yeah. That sums it up. I like . . . that." She shoves out a hand to Sancha. "I'm Chavez. She's Zhong."

"Sancha. And Don." She holds Chavez's hand and eyes a second too long. "You live here?"

"No. Sorry. We're just in town for a short-term assignment."

"Like rocket scientists out at the NASA center, planning a trip to Mars?"

Chavez makes a sound like a laugh, if she laughed. "Well. Yeah. I guess. Kind of like that."

Zhong interrupts. "We can't discuss our work."

#

Zhong and Chavez walk back into the command center just as Pilgrim steps up to the podium, shoving aside a man pointing at the middle screen with a laser pointer. "Cheech and Chong. Glad you could join us. Finally."

Chavez opens her mouth but Zhong speaks first. "Coffee's here." She smiles sweetly. "Only the best for America's finest."

A couple of men in the back jump up and head for them, but the man with the laser pointer dances a red dot on the floor in front of them.

"Gentlemen, we have work."

He uses the red dot to herd them back to their seats like a couple of cats.

"Afterward, coffee. You're going to need it."

He turns back to the screen.

"We have unimpeachable intel that a major player has a safe house approximately 6.7 kilometers from here. Tonight, we're going to hit that house with everything we've got: assault vehicles, choppers, Special Forces, you name it. We're going to take that place apart. Anyone there will be choppered out and taken to a secret location on a base on a communist island in the Caribbean. If you see an item like this . . .," he put the red dot on the side screen with the hat box that holds the bomb, ". . . do not touch. Contact your superior, who will make arrangements for our explosive techs to secure the device."

"All of you." He pauses and glares at the women. "All of you who considered ops briefings important enough to attend, have your assignments." He pauses, and the men twist sideways into starting positions in their seats. "And now you may have your coffee."

The room explodes and men swarm the coffee trays the women are holding. A lot of coffee sloshes onto the floor but some stays in the cups. One man, the biggest and the fastest, holds his cup up to his lips and the room freezes to watch his reaction.

His face twists like a bad special effect.

"Hoo-whee. That's the worst coffee I've ever had."

Chavez whispers, "Yes!" to Zhong.

Another man takes a sip. "That must have been filtered through the ass-end of a skunk."

Everyone joins in.

"That tastes worse than my ex-wife."

"I agree, that does taste worse than your ex-wife."

"I've drunk piss out of a foxhole better than this."

But they are grinning and making faces. And drinking more.

The big one raises his cup to them. "I believe you girls are our permanent baristas."

"Or sewage engineers."

Cups are raised to the women.

"More."

"Shit." Chavez hisses at Zhong. "I'm getting out of here before the fart-sniffing contest starts."

She turns and marches out. Zhong pauses and studies the address on the board:

504 Greendale.

day four: 10:00 a.m.

find your castle

Since Sancha has gone to class, Dulce and I leave DB in charge of the Q and head out. She barely makes it to the curb before she needs to sit down and rest, and I wonder if we can make the two blocks to where DB says the castle is. But she gives me a wan smile and reaches up for my hand after only a minute's rest. I pull her up and she leans into me. There is a sour smell to her, like someone who hasn't seen a shower in days, and I'm reminded that, indeed, queens and royalty often went some time without bathing. I breathe in again and realize that smelling is just my body sampling Dulce's body and incorporating it into my own. My attitude adjusts and I feel honored to share her air. Looked at that way, her scent seems complex and . . . beautiful, in its own way. I put my arm around her and hold her as tight as I can without crushing her.

She says, "I can make it with you, Don."

I'm filled with a new strength from her confidence in me. She's smiling that regal smile again. How can she give me so much joy, and still smile like she's the one getting joy from it? I wonder if maybe there is something in royal blood that makes this woman better than the best of us, better even than an angel.

It feels like we take only a single step, staring into each other's eyes, and we're at the palace.

This doesn't look like a palace. Rotting Victorian house, thigh-high weeds, a white sign that I can't read. I smile at Dulce. She seems at home here, so maybe this is the palace. I learn again that real royalty has real modesty. We help each other up the steps, leaning on each other more than we need to. She giggles and I laugh.

There is no one at the receptionist desk. (Palaces have reception desks nowadays? One of many developments I missed out on.) We sit on the couch and she leans her head on my shoulder.

Next thing I know someone is shaking me awake. The shaker is a thin man with lines and pock marks on his pale face.

"You can't sleep here," he says. His voice carries the sad resignation of a thousand rainy days. He looks at Dulce, who is barely breathing, and his face takes on a panicked expression. I reach up and stroke her cheek and she purrs awake.

"Thank God," he says. "OK, I'm glad you can wake up, but you can't stay here. I'm very, very sorry, but you can't. We can lose our license working with unauthorized clients."

I smile at the joy he's going to feel when he recognizes her as a queen.

"No. We're here to . . . return Dulce to where she belongs."

"Where she belongs?"

I nod.

"Ah. Come on back to intake."

day four: 10:30 a.m.

no room at the inn

The scarred floorboards creak and moan as we walk down the hall to a room with peeling paint and a fading couch that faces an overstuffed chair just like mine at home. He gestures us to the couch and settles into the chair.

Dulce puts her head on my shoulder. Her trust warms a smile from me. The man sees my smile and gives it back. He reaches out a hand to me.

"My name's Don," he says.

My mouth hangs open. "That's my name." I wonder if we're related. No, I'm not that spacey. I know that shared last names denote familial relation. But maybe our first names denote some astral commonality. In any case, I feel a bond, like I'm talking to myself.

Other Don releases my hand. "I see that she is comfortable with you. Is she comfortable coming here?"

I don't want to lie to myself. "She's agreed to come back, but I think she likes the street. And free Mountain Dew."

A look of concern rolls across his face and I mimic it to keep our shared face in sync. He lets it slide.

"Sometimes that's enough. Judging from her appearance, she seems to need our services. We are fortunate to have some very good people here to help her. Not much money, but good people. Ironically, in some ways, the more they cut our funding, the better our people become."

"It must be an honor to serve royalty."

He thinks about it. "It is. Put them back on their thrones. I like your attitude."

"That's why we're here."

He pauses, studying her. Her breath becomes shallower against my throat, and he notices that and looks worried.

"And your relationship to her is what, exactly?"

"She is a queen and I serve her."

He decides he has heard worse explanations. Apparently, we Dons are good at accepting.

"But she is willing to commit herself, at least for evaluation?"

"She is looking forward to returning."

We have that concerned look on our faces again. He stands up and goes behind a metal desk with an old computer.

"Then let's get . . . what is her name?"

"Dulce."

"Let's get Dulce checked in, and we'll start treating her like a queen deserves."

I'm glad that another Don will be here for her. I feel warm and good.

"What is her full name?"

I'm surprised that I don't know.

"Just Dulce. I don't know the rest."

He looks up from the computer and studies my face. Decides to let this slide, too. He points at the small fanny pack that she carries.

"I can't open that myself, but you can. Perhaps there's a wallet in there, insurance card, something that might help us."

I nod and unzip the bag. There's not much in it. A couple of Quick Stop wet wipes. Sugar packets. She sure has a jones for that stuff.

"Here." I pull out a driver's license and offer it to Other Don.

"No insurance card?"

I shake my head.

"Well, let's see what we can do with this."

He types away and his face brightens. "Miss Dulcinea—that's her formal name—was here two years ago. Before my time, but the staff agreed with you that she was royalty. They loved her."

Dulcinea. I love this. A name fit for a queen.

"That makes me feel good about the people here. This is the right place for her."

He nods with a concerned frown. "None too soon. She appears to be slipping away."

"It's been an hour since she had her last Mountain Dew."

He studies me and says, "Yes. Let's see if we can get our queen a bed."

I realize that I've only seen Dulcinea sleep on concrete.

"You're very kind." This is a good Don, and I'm very proud of us.

He types, frowns, types some more, frowns some more. When he looks up, his eyes are wet.

"There's nothing."

"I know. Dulcinea has been living with nothing to enhance her humility. It is wonderful that you will return her to privilege. I think you, too, are an angel."

He blushes, bites our lip.

"No. You don't understand. I've got nothing. Dulcinea has no insurance. There used to be federal programs, but . . ."

His voice trails off.

I encourage this remarkable man. "You are doing this all on your own? I can only aspire to someday reach the greatness of your heart."

"No. You don't understand." He breathes hard and looks away. "There used to be programs. We told them how bad addiction is, how many tries at rehab it takes for people to shake these demons. But they rejected that. The new administration decided that good people don't need help. If you need help, you don't deserve it. Kind of a national catch-22. They give people three shots at rehab. Three strikes, and you're out." He pointed at the computer. "Dulcinea's had two stays at other centers since she was here. She's out."

What he was saying sinks in.

"You're telling me you have no room, even though you think she needs help?"

"Desperately. And we can't give it."

He breathes hard and it makes me realize how soft and shallow Dulcinea's breathing is.

"Can't you—"

"I got fired from my last job for trying to sneak someone in. I can't lose this one. Besides, we're talking about federal law. I could go to prison."

"This doesn't make sense. You're telling me we can afford a prison bed for a good Don but not a bed for a queen?"

"Prisons are all for profit now."

He looks at me a long time. "Get her help. You may need these." He hands me a stack of three cards. I look at them. They are for funeral homes.

I'm outraged. "You're telling me the only help we've got is help dying?"

"The same federal programs cover burial expenses. Most customers don't need three strikes there."

I stand up and point a finger at . . . something. "We won't even help a dying queen in trouble? I do not like this country, I find now. I think I would blow it all to smithereens if I could."

day four: noon

a spoonful of sugar

DB is heartbroken when I return with Dulcinea. Heartbroken, and defeated. We ease her into a folding chair by the drink fountain and hand her a drink.

I say, "DB, why don't you take Dulcinea to my house around the corner? Both of you get some real sleep."

He looks at her. She's tired, but drinking.

"You got Mountain Dew at home?"

"No. You can take a couple of bottles from here. I'll pay for them."

He thinks about it. "This place is kind of becoming home for her. I don't have to tell you, we've hit rock bottom. I tried something with Dulce that I thought would help, adding sugar to her stuff to maybe wean her off, but maybe it's made her crash more. I don't know. I don't know what we can do if we can't get her into some kind of rehab. I sure don't know what I can do on my own. But just coming inside here is a step up." He looks around, snorts, then says, "Yeah. Like a home." Another snort. "Sort of. So if you don't mind, we'll stay here a while."

I smile. "We are at your service."

"And I'm at yours. Oh, I couldn't figure out how to work the cash register. I just put out a plastic bucket and a sign."

"We had customers?"

"A couple."

DB lies down at Dulcinea's feet and goes to sleep.

I walk to the counter and see DB's hand-painted sign: PAY WHAT YOU CAN. Inside is a handful of change and a Denny's coupon.

Sancha comes in, hours early. She dumps her books on the counter and looks at the bucket with me.

"Good idea."

"Wasn't really an idea, just a mistake. Maybe we should run it by the owner."

"The owner who hasn't answered emails or phone calls for years? Yeah, right. I send the receipts in every day, man. This place has been losing money for years. He won't notice."

I have a blurry image of an angry man who we don't want to cross. "Maybe. But he might."

"No, man. Look at this place. What owner has a convenience store that doesn't sell gas? Can't make money like that.

"Don, you don't understand America now. We got so many tariffs and trade wars, there ain't no way to make honest money by making something of value anymore. But we got so many tax breaks for corporations, that the way to make money is to lose a hundred dollars and get back a thousand on taxes. Why I'm studying to be an accountant. Trust me, man, I can send in statements that will make the owner a happy and rich man."

My head hurts, but I have more important things to do than think about my head.

I look at Dulce and DB, think about what they deserve and what they get. Probably a lot of people out there like them. Maybe pay-as-you-can is worth a try.

A beat-down woman comes in dragging a kid. She picks out a box of Twinkies and a quart of milk and brings it to the counter.

Maybe we should provide nutrition guidance to the community.

"You know," I say. "Things like milk are cheaper at the Publix up on Whitesburg. They've got fresh produce," I smile at the kid, "and their ice cream is good, too."

"Yeah. If'n you got a car and money for gas to get there. We live on what you sell here."

The bell dings and a tall man with glasses and a suit comes in and takes a cup of coffee. He stands in what he thinks is a line behind the woman. I half expect him to complain about being held up by poor people talking, but he just smiles.

The woman says, "How much?"

I point at the sign.

"I ain't looking for charity."

"Isn't charity. Prices everywhere are pretty arbitrary. Like I said, for years, Publix has been charging less, and places like this charge more because our customers are too poor to complain. We're just flipping the flex in the system around in people's favor. Next week, when your luck turns, come back and pay more."

She pulls money out of her pocket. "I brought enough money, but if I pay a little less, I can pay some to the woman who babysits him. I'm way behind with her."

I take half out of her hand and leave the rest.

"Bless you." She and the boy leave.

The tall man blinks behind his glasses.

"I'd heard about places like this. Didn't know we had any in Huntsville."

I'm not sure what he means. There are lots of convenience stores here. But I nod and he keeps talking.

"I pass this place every day on my way to the genetics center where I work. Never thought of stopping until you painted the outside."

Sancha and I look at each other. I say, "Atlas?" and Sancha shrugs.

"Maybe I'll start coming by for my coffee."

The man takes a sip and makes a face.

"Maybe tomorrow I'll bring you some coffee beans I've got from Sumatra."

He puts a bill that neither of us recognize in the bucket and walks out.

Sancha says, "Didn't know Ben Franklin was on money."

"Better get out your computer and check it out."

We walk outside to see the paint job.

"No paint," says Sancha.

"No. But no spider webs over the Quick Stop sign, either. Atlas must have wiped them off. And replaced the light outside."

"Boy's got ambition."

I go back inside and look at Dulcinea and DB sleeping in the corner. If the rich guy can help, I can, too. I slide DB's backpack away from him, open it, and take out Dulcinea's sugar bag. Almost empty. I take it to the shelves, open a box of sugar, and fill Dulcinea's bag with it.

DB shouldn't have to pay for Dulcinea's drug of choice, even if it's just sugar.

day four: 2:00 p.m.

maybe all of you forgot

I look out the window and see Harriette leaning on the glass, unmoving. For a moment I think she's died there and I worry that I have lost a friend. I count: I've only got five friends that I know of. Wonder how many friends most people have? I'll ask Sancha to look it up when I get a chance.

But Harriette's not dead; she's just Harriette. Slowpoke. She usually looks half-dead. Except for her eyes. I can see they're moving, as always. She's looking at the line of customers at the unmanned counter, paying and checking out on their own with no clerk. She looks at DB and Dulcinea.

I walk outside and she straightens up. She looks at me and I see a flicker of a smile try to come out of her tired cop face, and then quickly fade. I smile, and hold my smile for both of us.

Her mouth opens, a little. "Got a complaint. Why I'm here."

"Our windows are too dirty? Dulcinea washed them, sort of, but they're still too streaky."

"No, they're fine. Not my department anyway." She looks down at her shoes. "Neither is what I was sent here for. Guy complained that he stopped by this morning and you weren't charging people. Said you were guilty of communism. Stupid stuff. But he's on the chamber of commerce. He went to the mayor, the mayor called the police chief, who called somebody, who called somebody, which wound up with me standing in my lieutenant's office explaining that there's no law against giving stuff away and my lieutenant telling me, 'Find one.'"

Sancha walks in on the end of that.

"Jesus, man, even you know that's bullshit."

She gets in Harriette's face. No reaction from Harriette. She gets closer.

"Like we ain't got enough real problems that you police are closing your eyes to, so you got time for this."

Harriette's face twitches.

"Not my choice. My job."

"Job of a cop or a lackey?"

Harriette's eyes catch fire, like embers that had been smoldering for years finally catching.

"You think I don't know? You think I don't *know*? I was once a hot-headed punk like you, swore to serve and protect. Not to kiss ass. Not to serve the thin blue line. You know what's going on while I'm wasting my time over here?"

She stabs an angry finger out in the neighborhood.

"Three blocks that way, there's a cathouse. Not just a cathouse, but a cathouse of sex slaves from China and Russia. If you go there and stand in the front door and talk to the scared girl who answers in her underwear, as soon as you show the badge, she'll lose her fake smile and stare down at the floor. Then rough-looking guys will appear behind her and tell you the police have no power here. And the girl will be too scared to cross the threshold of the door and come with you. Afraid if she crosses it, bad things will happen.

"And she's right. You want to tell her not to be afraid, that it's safe to talk to you. You're law and order. But you know if she talks, and you bust the place, the owner will bail his boys out in an hour and be on the phone with the mayor complaining that this was just an Amway meeting for Asian women and you've interfered with a legitimate business that brings money into the city."

Now Harriette gets into Sancha's face.

"The lawyers will make money, the owner will buy the mayor a nice dinner with a campaign check, and you'll lose your stripes. And the girl? She'll wind up in a dumpster. When they fish her out, there'll be a two-inch article in the back of the paper. And somebody high up will say, 'illegal immigrant. Broke the law and got what she deserved.'"

"Harriette, that sounds like a bad TV show."

She looks away from me.

"Ask any cop. We can't stand up, any more than she can. Any more than you can, even in little things. Stay in line."

Sancha says, "Hell, no."

Harriette gives her a long, sad look.

"At least don't get hurt. Print up some fake receipts. Tell people to take them so they can prove that nothing good happened here. Don't be brave."

"Brave?" I yell. "Brave? This is supposed to be America, the land of the brave. What happened? We were big enough to admire men as different as John Wayne and Sitting Bull, Robert E. Lee and Nat Turner. All because they were heroes and stood up and howled."

They both look at me.

Harriette says, "Never heard you so loud."

I realize I've been shouting in an un-angel voice. I try a calmer tone. "Never heard you talk so much."

Sancha says, "For a man who's forgotten everything, you sure do remember a lot."

I pause and think about it. "Maybe I didn't forget. Maybe everyone else did."

day four: 6:00 p.m.

all in the wrists

Sancha flops down in my one living room chair and fiddles with the TV remote.

"Told you, man, no such things as ghosts."

I look at my chair and remain standing.

"Not ghosts, Sancha. Just kind of a weird vibe here. Feeling, maybe. Want to see if you get it, too."

"Only vibe I've got, man, is that I can't make your TV work." She puts the remote down on the side table and stands up. "I don't know, man. Only a fool runs their life on feelings. You use your brain, you think, you learn what the world's trying to teach you, and you live on that."

"I'll try. But can I get you to just walk around, see if anything seems strange to you?"

She gives me a pitiful look. "You mean like Feng shui? Analyze your house to see if you would get better energy if you pointed your bed different? Don't know much about that."

"Not looking for what you know. Just walk around and tell me what you feel."

She puts out her arms, closes her eyes and slowly spins around. "Ommmm." Opens her eyes.

"I see a really tiny room, maybe eight by eight. One chair with a side table, facing a not-so-new TV. Nothing on the walls." She walks around the chair. "No books, no magazines. The table has a couple of scratches; the chair is old. But both of them clean. The whole room's clean." She laughs. "How does a dude who keeps his home like this work at the Q? No wonder you got a bug for cleaning. Seriously, you mop this place down every night?"

"No." I feel embarrassed, like being caught trying to be the teacher's pet. But she's right. Every morning, the last thing I do is wash the sheets, mop the floors, and wipe down every surface. Lock the door behind me, check it twice, then wipe down the doorknob. Doesn't everybody?

I follow her into the hall. She pauses a second, then takes a right.

"Why?" I ask.

"You said to check things out."

"No. I mean, why right and not left?"

She thinks about it.

"You don't ask the expected questions."

I shrug.

I get a smile from her. "You know, I'd never thought about it. I'm left-handed by nature, so you'd think I'd go left. But my old man—he was Chicano." She raises a fist. "Chicanos rule.

Anyway, he was right-handed, and I always wanted to be like him. Is that weird? Mom was black, which was cool, too. But it never seemed to matter much to her, so we thought we were a Chicano family because it mattered to Papa.

"So I guess that's it. You're born one way, look around and the world makes you something else. Maybe the two fight forever. Maybe you just learn to go right."

So we go right into the kitchen.

"Spartan," she says.

She walks across the floor to the refrigerator. Opens the door, looks in and turns to give me a sad look.

"You know, you can keep stuff in here, other than that one water bottle. Food. Beer. Essentials."

"I know." It does strike me as an unnecessarily messy idea. But I don't say that.

She closes the door. "Same thing as the living room. Looks temporary. You've been at the Q as long as I've been there. Did you just move in here?"

I think about it. "I don't think so. Feels like . . . forever."

"Who do you pay rent to?"

I open my hands. "Don't know."

"Well, that'll take care of itself. When they come to throw you out, ask them who they are. Even ask them who you are."

"Certainly. But I mean, what kind of feeling do you get in this room?"

"Clean?"

On the way out, I stop her at the little half-door.

"How about now?"

I get another curious look. "I don't know. Feels like I'm half in a bare kitchen, half in a bare hall."

"Close your eyes."

She does. "Now I feel like I'm going to open my eyes and find you standing there with a butcher knife with blood on it."

"Open them. Take a step back into the kitchen. What now?"

"Now I realize that I'm safe, because you'd have to clean up the mess. Maybe have to send me a thank you note for being the guest of honor at your murder party."

"Smart ass."

We inventory the bathroom and the two bed-rooms. Sancha still won't admit that she feels anything. I take her back to the half-door.

"You're telling me that you don't feel anything here?"

She looks at me, looks at the door, looks at the wall. Taps on the wall, steps out into the hall where she can see into the bathroom and the kitchen at the same time.

"There's a gap." She points at the hall between the two. "Small one. Maybe a small closet."

I look where she's pointing and see that she's right.

Now *I* get the image of a crazy slasher.

"Why would I have a closet with a half-door painted shut?"

She steps back into the kitchen, squats down and examines the door. Looks at me and then reaches out her hand.

The door opens for her with no effort.

My stomach does a flip-flop, like when a roller coaster starts to drop uncontrollably. Behind the door there's a set of rickety, wooden stairs leading down into a screen of cobwebs.

"C'mon," she says.

"No."

"Suit yourself." She turns around and backs in.

"I'll get a flashlight. And a knife. In case."

"No need." I hear a snap and the hole is filled with light. She disappears. "Looks like maybe an old-time root cellar. Not much room. Concrete walls, dirt floor."

I ask a question I don't think I want an answer to. "What's down there?"

"Not much." I hear a thump, then several more. "Nothing, really. Just a bunch of cardboard moving boxes. All feel empty. All new, like they just came from a Home Depot."

It still scares me. "Come out, please, Sancha."

Her face pops out, followed by her body.

"Nothing to be scared of, man."

"Fine." I suddenly want to be out of here. "Let's go back to that 504 Greendale house, see if any-one's come back."

"Tomorrow. I don't want to walk all the way out there tonight. Let's just go in the living room and watch the tube. I call dibs on the chair. Guess we'll just have to drink water tonight. Tomorrow, let's get some beer from the Q."

Great. More stuff to wipe down every day.

day four: 10:00 p.m.

as long as the good guys win

Chavez and Zhong stand outside the TEDAC and take in the North Alabama night.

"Pretty here," said Zhong.

Chavez takes an unlit cigarette out of her mouth. She gave up smoking on a health kick a few months back but couldn't break the habit of sneaking outside to smoking zones and using a cigarette for a prop.

The night is quiet and still, until a line of black Cadillac Escalades appear on the road leading in. The gate guard steps out of his shack and waves them through. The Escalades are standard issue for the security services that guard Washington nobles—that is, politicians—above a certain level. Since Bob Pilgrim is here incognito, the Escalades all have magnetic pizza delivery logos on the black paint.

Chavez says, "People must think there's one hell of a pizza party somewhere."

"I think I'd buy stock in Little Joe's Pizza if I saw that train pulling into a bar."

The line stops in unison with the middle vehicle at the door. Men in dark suits and dark glasses jump out into the dark night and form a human funnel into the building. Every other man stands at attention while the companions on his left and right scan the horizon for any threat they can see at night through their sunglasses.

The door opens and Bob Pilgrim half-falls out. He vomits on the ground, laughs, and steps out over the puddle.

Zhong whispers. "His clothes are a mess, he is stepping over a pile of his own puke, but every white hair on his head is still perfectly in place. Think it's a wig?"

"No. You're thinking of his boss."

"No. I was not thinking of that. Ever."

Pilgrim walks up to them with a big smile.

"Cheech and Chong. What happened? Did the boys throw you out?"

He laughs.

"No sir. They went home a couple of hours ago. We thought someone should stay here."

"Those boys deserve a break. They had a hard day."

"Did you think what we . . ." The emphasis on "we" was slight, but Zhong still elbowed her. ". . . what *we all* did today will help?"

"Of course. I wouldn't have ordered it otherwise."

"Yes, sir."

He stumbles past them.

As he gets to the door, Zhong says, "Sir, could I ask you something?"

With some difficulty, he turns with a politician's smile. "Of course."

"I was looking at the Maximum Aw Shit radius, sir."

"Impressive, isn't it?"

"Yes, sir, it is."

"That's why I have a fast air force jet fueled up and waiting at the airstrip. One hint that the bomb's about to blow, and I'm out of here. Someone's got to stay alive to command."

"Yes, sir. But how will the bomb be detonated, sir?"

He holds onto the door jamb, but speaks like a man used to giving speeches, even while drunk. "Two ways. There's a remote control that will work when the bomb is out of the box. Fortunately, we have that remote secured. Otherwise, you can turn the beads on the necklace to spell out GO^USAxx. Each time you get a letter right, the necklace flashes to let you know that you got it right. After the last letter, a timer starts for the number of hours the last two digits are set for. We chose that code because only an idiot would choose that, and everybody knows we're not idiots, so they wouldn't guess that."

"Yes, sir. But, the range of the weapon. I did a few calculations. If the bomb can destroy that much, then the shock waves and the fallout beyond MAS will destroy most of the world."

He grins and stands up straighter.

"Teach people to respect the Great American Republic, won't it? Don't mess with the USA."

With a fist bump and a hoo-rah, he stumbles into the building.

day five: 8 a.m.

i swear this is where i left it

It's a beautiful new day, and I'm determined to put the fears of yesterday behind me.

Sancha stayed over on the cot in the second bedroom. I lay awake all night terrified of something. Sancha? Of course not. Something from the root cellar? The pucker in my nether regions tells me that's it.

But what? A cardboard box monster? Sancha's right, we learn about the ways of the world and that's what makes us what we are. I've lost that somehow.

Time to rebuild myself, based on facts. I repeat, "There are no cardboard box monsters."

The pucker is not convinced, but I'll keep working on him. The mind is stronger than the asshole.

I hope.

In the morning, we check in at the Q. Atlas is using crates of milk to do curls while a couple of customers are arguing over the pay bucket.

Sancha says, "Man, I was afraid of this. Everybody's trying to make the other guy pay."

I walk over. A black woman with two young kids in tow is shaking her fist at the suit guy from yesterday.

"I pay my own way." She drops a handful of wadded-up bills and change in the bucket. "Don't you tell me you've got me covered."

"No, I . . . Sorry. I meant no offense. I'm just trying to help out. I like this place and want to see it succeed." He sees me and pushes a burlap coffee bag at me. "See if you don't like this better than the coffee you've been serving."

The woman hands her bag to one of the kids. "Sorry, mister. Didn't mean to snap at you. Just seems that sometimes you fancy pants alternate between slapping people down and pretending to help. And keeping this place alive is a hell of a lot more important to me than you."

"I get it. How about you pay your way, and I still put in the extra I was going to pay?"

"Good." She turns to me, sees my Q shirt. "Maybe you can use that extra money to get some fruits and vegetables in here, replace some of the soda and pork rinds?"

Atlas looks at me and I nod.

Sancha says, "Ain't going to find none of that in the catalog the owner gives us to order from."

The three of us look at each other and burst out laughing at the same time.

"The owner, yeah, right. He cares."

"Tell you what," says Sancha. "How about we do this from now on? There's the Quick Stop, and there's the Q. Every day, I'll make up a statement for the Quick Stop, and send it to the owner. But we take the money out of the bucket and run the Q. Get what we want in here."

I say, "Eventually he'll catch on."

We look at each other again and laugh some more.

I look at Atlas. "How about this? Sancha and I need to run an errand. After we get back, you take some cash and get some produce from Publix?"

The woman at the counter shakes her head. "Go to the farmers' market. Cheaper and better, but harder for a lot of us to get to."

"OK, Atlas, we're heading out. Can you cover while we're gone?"

He frowns and flexes his arms.

"Ah. You don't want to miss the gym. How about, while we're gone, you get a workout by shoving the racks around to make room for the new stuff? Maybe even set up a rack for that protein stuff you guys eat and drink to make your muscles big?"

He grins and points both hands at me like pistols and flicks his thumb down to fire them at me.

I take that as a good thing. Maybe.

Sancha and I walk up to 504 Greendale, see if we can learn anything new.

"Man, we still gotta get a car or something. These walks are killing me."

"Cars are expensive. Pain in the butt, too. Insurance, maintenance, and you've got to buy air fresheners and those little fuzzy dice." I wonder how I know technical things like this, but I do.

"Yeah. You're right. I don't know. Horses, maybe? Think how cool that would be, Don and Sancha of the Q riding stallions on a quest for glory, like something from another time."

"Maybe." I haven't seen a lot of horses around town. Any, actually. But what do I know? Maybe she's right. "Sancha, I got another problem. Dulcinea can't get into the palace."

"Dulcinea? The palace? Oh yeah, that kind of palace. When you going to learn, man?"

I feel my lips tightening. "Some things I don't want to learn."

"OK, that's cool. But it is tough out there, man. Used to be, people thought that the more addicts—royalty—we fixed up and returned to the world, the better off we'd all be. Now, the rulers—the real royalty—think the best solution for anybody who is inconvenient in their America is to eat shit and die. That's what they want for royalty like Dulce, gays, lesbians, closet Democrats, black folks, Hispanic." She stops. "Damn. No wonder I sometimes feel out of place. I'm on all their lists. Fuck 'em." She pauses at the street corner and looks up at the sky. "Don't know what to do about Dulce. But I know a guy who can help us with transport, after we get done here."

We turn onto Greendale and I'm still looking at the sky when Sancha stops dead and I crash into her since she's always a half-step ahead.

"What the . . ." I catch myself and realize it's the first time I've almost cursed. Or even been irritated enough to want to. Must be a cranky street.

I look where she's pointing. There's an empty lot.

"We're on the wrong street," I say.

Sancha points at the street sign. Points at the numbers on the curb. 502, blank space, 506.

I look at her.

"504 Greendale is gone."

day five: 10:00 a.m.

gone, gone, gone

I don't mean that 504 Greendale has been swept away in a tornado, leaving a pile of rubble. I mean gone. Like it never was. The lot is all grass with a for sale sign in the middle of it. No foundation, no outline, no driveway.

Nothing to see here. Move along.

"Sancha, you remember, don't you?"

"I remember."

"That was what, two days ago?"

"Yeah. Might as well have been forever, like time skipped a beat and we're in a different world now."

I feel uneasy. "Kind of like what happened to me."

She looks at me. "No, man. You're going to be fine in a couple of days or so. What you got is some kind of brain flu or something, man. You been eating one of those caveman diets or something? I heard you can get some kind of brain fog from that."

"No. I eat tacos and doughnuts. And drink beer with you."

"Nothing wrong with that. Twenty-first century All-American diet. Food for a normal man."

I swallow and my voice cracks. "Maybe I'm not an angel. Maybe a lot of things are going on."

"Maybe. But I'll tell you what. Before Monday you were a son-of-a-bitch, man. Now you're a good man. An ordinary man, but good." She looks out at the bare lot. "What happened to you is not like this, man. Not the same. We got to find out what happened here."

She looks up and down the street. No sign of life, no kids playing or old men watering lawns. Houses, but as quiet as the lot we're in front of. "That way." She walks off to the house on the left, and I follow. We crowd together on the table-sized concrete stoop and she knocks on the door.

Nothing. I reach around and rap on the window.

Nothing. If there's a cockroach in there, he's not talking.

Next two houses, same. At the third house, Sancha taps on the door and there's a sound of hurried footsteps, then silence. We stand there awhile, knocking and calling out hello, but no one comes to the door. We're four houses down and across the street before we hear the sound of children's voices. I've given up and am just staying in the street while she knocks, but the noise catches my attention. The door cracks open and I look to see the timid face of a Hispanic woman, small like Sancha, whispering something to her.

Excited, I skip up to the porch behind Sancha. The woman in the house suddenly looks panicked.

Sancha says, "This is my friend Don." She looks at my shirt. "Don Q."

A large man appears behind the woman. He gives me a look of shock, says something in a torrent of Spanish, and slams the door.

Sancha is staring at me.

"Sancha, what did he say?"

"You don't want to know, man. Didn't call you an angel."

I knock on the door. "Let me introduce myself to them. People like me when they get a chance to meet me."

She takes my hand.

"Don't think so, man."

She drops my hand and stands there, thinking for a minute.

"Let me try this on my own, in Spanish. You go back to 504 and work down the other way. Meet me at the lot in half an hour."

I walk away. At 504, I look back. Sancha has disappeared inside.

I knock on silent house doors until I'm out of sight of 504, and then walk back. I stand at the empty lot for another half-hour before Sancha reappears.

I call out, "Hey, where'd you go?"

She walks past me with her head down.

"Walk, man, walk. We got to get out of this neighborhood."

She takes off and I catch up. It's hard to talk while we're walking this fast, but I try.

"Not now," she says.

Finally, we pass a schoolyard, kids playing and teachers trying to pretend they're in charge. We get past it and see a car backing out of a driveway and a couple walking a dog.

"OK," she says. "Keep walking, but let's talk."

"So they told you what happened there? We weren't crazy?"

"Not sure the whole world hasn't gone crazy, man. But they aren't crazy, just scared. They say a real bad man used to live there. But that ain't what scares them. Here's the story they told.

"Sometime around midnight last night. Last night, man. They say they woke up to a helicopter above the street, and bright lights everywhere. Then came a bunch of helicopters and Humvees and heavy equipment, men in black coveralls with no logo except the American flag. They start taking the house apart piece-by-piece, wrapping every-thing up in plastic, and taking it away in a string of eighteen-wheelers. Toward the end, the husband got the nerve to walk down to talk to somebody. He wanted to ask if the bad man who lived there was finally getting arrested, 'cause he wanted to testify.

"The government man told him nothing was happening here and if he told lies about something happening, they'd come back and shoot his ass for treason. He went back home. In a couple of hours, everything was gone and the street looked like it is now. Said they called the consolidated TV-and-newspaper-and-internet news site. As soon as he gave the address he was told, 'Nothing happened there. Fake news.' The family hasn't opened their door since. Says they're leaving soon as they can."

She stopped. I thought she was trying to catch her breath, but she was staring at me.

"He said the bad man, he looked like you."

day five: noon

brain science

"I ain't saying you're a bad man, Don," says Sancha, without breaking stride. "You're not. Not even sure the guy in the house was saying that. Said you looked like the bad man."

I grab her arm and we stand there in the street kicking that around for a few minutes. Finally, she says, "Look, man, this is getting us nowhere and we got bigger problems. I got an idea how to solve our transportation problem."

"Yeah, and I've got to find a way to get Dulcinea back to the palace."

"You're not going to give up on that royalty bit, are you? Look, I've also got an idea about something that might help Dulce. It's a long shot."

"Better than no shot. What you got?"

"There's this guy. Don't know how to explain him, but he might be able to help. Or not."

"Good enough. Tell me where to find him. I'll go to him and you run your errand."

#

Now I stand outside the building Sancha sent me to, staring for a long time trying to figure it out. It is a round building from the sixties, back when Huntsville tried to build everything to look modern and science fiction-y. The front door has an old marble sign with JIM TROY, NEUROLOGIST chiseled into it. "Neurologist" is painted over, except that you can still read it. One third of the way around the building there is a handmade door with a hand-painted sign that reads, POSITIVITY THERAPY. I kept circling. Half-way between the two doors someone has knocked a hole in the wall and covered it with a tie-died flap. Above the flap is an abstract eye with the word, "psychic" scrawled around it.

I stand there and wonder about Sancha. Clearly, this is not what a queen needs. Dulcinea might need a nutritionist, if there was one who specialized in ambrosia and other royal fare. Or Mountain Dew. But not a neurologist—if this guy is a neurologist. And nothing on Earth is as positive as Dulcinea's smile, so she doesn't need positivity therapy.

On the other hand, she needs something.

I open the flap and go in.

It is dark inside, lit only by a circle of candles around the outer wall. As my eyes adjust, I see a lot of the interior walls have been knocked down haphazardly to waist height. Some of them have four-by-four posts shoved against the ceiling to absorb the load the walls had held. Some were doing their job. Some were not. The ceiling sags.

Colorful paint has been thrown randomly on the floor, ceiling and walls, with words like peace, love, and live your dream painted on the ceiling. I think of all the words you could broadcast to the world, and these seem pretty good. I trust the man immediately.

And speaking of the man, there he is. Snoring on an old couch across from me, wearing a purple paisley robe with half the flap open over his bare, white ass. I look away and rap on a wooden bulletin board until he stops snoring, pulls down the robe, sits up, looks at me, and says, "Oh."

I walk over and say, "Sancha sent me."

He sits there smacking his lips and yawning until he figures out my sentence and his reply.

"Did Sancha send fifty dollars?"

I dig into my pocket and pull out the only thing there.

"She must have forgot. I only have five."

"Good enough." He takes the five. "Now, who do you need to see?"

"I don't know. What you got?"

"Is your problem neurological?"

So we're discussing me before Dulcinea. OK.

"Maybe."

He frowns.

"Are your problems psychological?"

"Maybe."

Another frown, but then a smile, when he spies an opportunity.

"Conventional wisdom has it that we start with the past and work forward. But I think the future is always the place of hope."

"Yes! There are so many wonderful things to see in the future."

"Good. Then let's start with a psychic reading. Our psychic is an extraordinarily generous spirit, who will happily do a reading for only five dollars. If need be, he can refer you to our therapist, who unfortunately must charge the full fifty dollars per session, because of insurance regulations. If he determines that a neurological exam is in order, he can recommend that. At a nominal fee."

"Fantastic! How soon can we see the future?"

day five: 1:00 p.m.

i see travel in your future

"Soon."

He smiles, stands up, and walks to a coat rack with a white lab coat and a scarf on it. He ignores the coat and winds the scarf around his head into a turban, and pulls an old wooden spool between the couch and a wooden chair that is draped in fake silk. On the spool is a wooden block with Jim Troy, Dr. Brainiac burned into it in a childish scrawl.

"Brainiac," I say.

He sweeps the block off the table and sits down in the chair.

"Kind of a joke, I guess. From my daughter, after I lost my license as a neurologist, and then turned to helping people as a therapist. Kind of a joke, because I will always work with brains. From my daughter." He pauses. "Back when she was speaking to me."

He reaches under the table and pulls out a blue and green glass globe. He sets it in the center, waves his hand around the base, and the globe glows like it is filled with tiny stars. He gestures at the couch and I take a seat where he had just been snoring. Snoring, and, I hoped, not drooling.

He rubs his hands over the globe. "I see you have recently made a wise decision that will result in future wealth and happiness."

"The decision to come here?"

He gives me a satisfied expression but refuses to answer me directly. He rubs the globe with my five-dollar bill.

"I see that, the more you put into this path, the more it will return."

"Well, it's not actually for me. I need to learn about a friend. A queen, actually."

He straightens up and gives me a sour look.

"You could have told me . . . Never mind. The winds of the future are here for everyone. A queen, you say?"

"Yes. She's currently visiting the convenience store where I work, living as a commoner."

"Ah. I see she is on sabbatical from the throne, conducting research in a place called the . . ." He studies my chest, then presses lightly on the globe with his fingertips. ". . . the Q."

"Yes! Yes! You really are . . . let me tell you more about Dulcinea."

"Not necessary. I already see beyond your surface knowledge. Dulcinea, queen from the land surrounded by waters."

"Yes. How do you know? Can you tell me this? Is there sugar in her homeland?"

"There is sugar. And milk and honey. It is a far, far better place."

"No wonder. Dulcinea seems to survive on nothing but sugar. Drinks Mountain Dew all day. Her brother, ah, servant, even carries a plastic bag of sugar that she sometimes needs to inhale through her nose to give her energy."

"Yes, I see. Then . . . wait, did you say her brother gives her sugar from a baggie for her to snort?"

"Yes. He's very kind."

"Are you sure it's just sugar?"

"Of course." I smile, modestly. "I even fill it up with sugar from the store so they won't have to pay for it themselves. Sancha says their kind of sugar is very expensive."

"So because of you, she's going to be snorting actual sugar?"

"Of course."

He takes his hands off the globe and looks at the ceiling. The dreamy smile is gone.

"I guess that probably won't hurt. Maybe. Hell of a way to quit, though. Tell me, though. Some queens have a royal tattoo, a series of dark dots on the inside of their elbows. Does Dulcinea have the royal mark?"

"Yes. On both arms. You really are psychic."

He turns off the globe and studies me.

"Not psychic. Just experienced with this kind of thing." He seems to make a decision.

"I see you are called by your queen—"

"Yes. Yes."

"—called to help her, today. The spirits say that you must get her to a drug counselor right now. It is very important to the whole . . . kingdom that she see someone as soon as you leave here."

"I tried that. We went to a center yesterday, and they said she had three strikes and they couldn't help her."

He looks very sad. He slowly unwinds the turban.

"Another tragedy. When I lost my certification as a neurologist, I got my counseling license. Lost that when I continued to work with a patient who had exceeded her allotment of treatment. Times are tough in the new America. Wasn't a whole lot better in the old one."

"Perhaps you could come and see her? I'd bring her here, but I don't think she'd make the walk."

He shook his head. "One violation treating an unapproved addiction and you lose your license. Two, and you go to jail, along with half the population who's there on one violation or another. She needs help, but I can't give it."

"I used to say, 'I can't' to callings before I became an angel."

"Well, I'm no angel."

He stands up.

I tell him. "I wasn't an angel before last Monday. Then I changed." I brighten. "Can you tell me what happened Monday?"

He seems to age a hundred years. "Don't ask me about last Monday, friend. Or next Monday. I'm a fraud. The only thing I know about any of those days ending in a 'y' is that they're going to be bad. You need to get out of all of this while you can."

"I think I did. Last Monday was when I awakened to my calling. I have no idea where or who I was before then. Just know that, now, I'm an angel with a mission. I was hoping you could help me with my past. After you help Dulcinea."

He studies me hard for a minute.

"So you must have been taking some fancy drugs yourself?"

"I don't think so. I don't know for sure, but it seemed that I was just standing in the Q and bang. Everything that I knew before was gone."

He sits back down and frowns.

"So, spontaneous amnesia?"

"Or a spiritual calling."

"Could be. There was some interesting work in permanent amnesia just before I left neurology. Do you mind if I ask you some questions about your experience?"

"I'll be glad to answer," I say. "If you'll come and see Dulcinea, too."

"No, I can't do—"

There is a loud banging on the main door.

"Police. Open up."

He stands up and heads for the flap.

"Let's go."

day five: 2:00 p.m.

even blind squirrels have visions

We cross into the ditch behind the odd building. I start to walk up the other side, but Dr. Brainiac turns and walks along the dry creek with his head bent down. I follow.

"Dr. Brainiac," I say.

"Just Jim. No, let's don't use that name anymore. Dr. Brainiac is fine."

"This isn't the way to the Q. I'd think you would know that."

He gives me a look like *are you kidding me* and keeps walking. Eventually we come up beside the junior high school and climb out behind the building. Then we cut through the hospital district back to the Q.

DB and Dulcinea are still on the floor when we get there. But there is something I have never seen here before: customers milling around. Many customers. There is a young boy in a Venom soccer shirt trying to reach over the sleeping pair for a drink.

"Here, let me help. What do you want?"

What he wants is something called a suicide, mixed to exacting specifications. Maybe we're going to have to hire a bartender for the fountain. I hand the completed achievement to him.

"It's on the house." I smile.

His mother pulls him away. "We pay our way, Mister. Our way, and a little more."

"Yes, ma'am."

Dr. Brainiac squats down, taking Dulcinea's pulse. He gives me a worried look.

"I can't tell if she's crashing or adjusting to all the sugar. I'm going to have to do some research to see if your sugar cure is crazy dangerous, or maybe it's doing some good, by luck. Sugar is at least a nutrient, even if it's a poor one. How long have you been cutting her stuff with it?"

"Oh, I just did that today. But DB says he's been giving her sugar for a long time."

DB says, "Not that long. I've tried cutting it with actual sugar for the last week to see if that would help. Maybe."

Dr. Brainiac stands up. "Well, we're going to have to get her out of here. Someplace with a little more privacy so I can really examine her and she can get some rest."

"My house?"

"That'd be great. You got a car we can use to take her?"

"No, we'll have to walk. It's not very far."

"I don't like the idea of her walking more than a few steps. I'm not sure how bad off she is right now."

"Sancha's working on transportation, but I don't know when she'll be back, or what she'll have."

Two guys lean over the couple to fill drinks. One of them almost drops his, but they recover and leave.

"I really think we need to get her out of here."

Atlas is here. "An idea. Maybe."

"Maybe's worth a shot."

Dr. Brainiac bends down and shakes her shoulder. No response.

I bend down and touch her shoulder lightly.

"Dulcinea."

Her eyes flutter open. She gives me that royal smile and the sunlight in my world doubles.

"I love it when you call me that. No one's called me that since I was a baby. I had forgotten."

"Dulcinea." We share a smile. "This is Dr. Brainiac."

He shakes his head about something and decides to let it go.

"He's going to help you."

"Can he get me a Mountain Dew?"

He bows. "Certainly, my queen."

While the doctor pours her a drink, Atlas runs behind the counter and gets the key. Runs out the door.

We get her up and follow Atlas next door. When I open the door to the dirty, empty laundromat, Dr. Brainiac says, "Wow." I wonder if that is a good wow or "wow, look at all those cobwebs" until he says, "Look at all this room."

"Someone might say, look at all this junk."

"Someone might say look at all of this treasure. Really, this place is the size of a basketball court."

"Used to be a lot of machines."

"Still a couple. Look, that wall still has two washers and two dryers. Wonder if they work?"

Atlas says, "Yeah." He points around the room to one thing after another. The doctor nods enthusiastically.

"The things we can do in here. We can make a room for DB and Dulcinea over there. Maybe one for me here. Room for other people who need help, if we can keep it quiet. Maybe an office. Maybe a kitchen."

I say, "I think you're getting ahead of yourself. I don't see a stove or even an old microwave in here."

"But look at what you do see: raw material everywhere."

Atlas points at his chest and says, "And Atlas."

Dr. Brainiac walks over to a stack of white sheets. Picks up the top one, shakes the dust off, and tugs at it. "These sheets are still strong. We can use them to make hammocks, get Dulcinea off of the floor."

I'm starting to see his vision. Maybe he *can* see the future. "Yeah. Make this something more than wasted space." Now I'm beaming. "A medical clinic over there. A rehab center here."

He hesitates, but his smile doesn't go away.

"Well, I don't know. I don't have a medical license anymore. We don't have drugs, supplies—"

"But we can do what we can do?"

He nods.

"And then maybe we can do a little more?"

He gives me a beat-down smile and points at the sheets.

"Maybe we could tie-dye these? Add a little color and hope?"

"That's it! You're on your own quest now. Make it shine."

Atlas nods again.

There is a series of high beeps outside. Sancha pulls into the parking lot, balanced on a hand-painted, black electric scooter with a bicycle seat, and leaning over to hold an identical one beside her. She has a big grin on her dirty face.

"Saddle up."

day five: 3:00 p.m

noble steeds

I think maybe I never rode on a scooter in my previous life. Maybe never even a bike. What looks perfectly natural when Sancha makes lazy donuts in the parking lot, showing off for the small crowd that's come out from the old Laundromat and the Q, is impossible for me.

I fall three times before the scooter moves. Really, who knew you had to tell a machine to stand upright?

But, like most things, this gets better with help and practice. I push the scooter to a side street with a downhill slant. Sancha directs Atlas and Dr. Brainiac to hold onto me from both sides while I coast down the hill, faster and faster. Like a commander of a fantastic rolling rocket ship, I push the throttle and blast off, pulling away from loving hands. The houses blur, the breeze grows into a gale roaring in my ears, and I'm afraid my steed and I are going to take off and fly.

I turn my head around and look back, grinning, wondering if Dulcinea can see me. I am basking in the glow of her imagined smile when the pavement hits me in the face.

They all run to me. Sancha gets there first. She pries my hand off the throttle, turns off the bike, and stops the little back wheel from spinning helplessly in the air. Brushes the gravel out of my face.

"Man," is what she says but her eyes are wet. "I'm going to get you a helmet. Maybe a full suit of armor, if you're going to ride like that."

"I know! I know! Wasn't that wonderful? Has any man ever travelled that fast in the history of travel?"

"Five miles an hour? Yeah, man, a few. But maybe, we'll limit you to that for a while. Just so you don't break the sound barrier or something."

I hop up, do a little dance, and pick up my steed.

"More!"

Sancha shakes her head.

"Don't know, man. Maybe this is enough for one day."

"Let me fly."

And that's what we do. We go up and down the street at fantastic speeds. I fall less and less, and when I do—despite meeting the ground with a violence that would rip a mortal man to shreds—my angelic nature protects me and I only get a few scrapes. Well, I get scrapes, bruises, cuts. A sore wrist. Throbbing head. But if this doesn't prove I'm an angel, nothing will. After I hit a tree and land on a rock wall, I bounce up grinning.

I wipe the blood out of my eyes and see Sancha staring at me.

"Man, I never seen nobody as bad at anything as you are at this. But I never seen nobody take a licking and keep on ticking like you. You sure—"

"More!"

She looks around and sees a scrap pile in a yard. She picks up a black-painted two-by-four about as long as she is tall.

She positions it on my lap.

"Driving with two hands doesn't seem to work for you. Try driving with one, hold this in the other for balance."

She shows me how to balance the two-by-four on the handlebar, clamping the wood with my hand while resting my thumb on the throttle.

It works. When I start to tip one way, the pole swings to the other side on its own, and pulls me back to the straight and narrow, like some cheerful bluebird in a Disney movie. It seems that, when your eyes are opened, everything in the world has its own will and magic, determined to help you on your mission.

Sancha points. "There. That place up ahead, that's the slave-house that Harriette was talking about."

I was expecting something like an Addam's family haunted house, but it looks like the other two-story duplexes in this neighborhood, maybe a little more faded, the paint peeling a little more. On the front porch a man sits drinking a beer. He is young and big, with muscles that stretch the arms of his shirt. His clothes look expensive, but he looks dirty.

Then my eyes shift gear and I see past the peeling paint and see the tortured women inside, looking like one of Hieronymus Bosch's paintings of a vision of hell.

I think of all of the bad things going on in there while I'm flying free out here. Doesn't seem right.

Sancha says, "Don't slow down."

day five: 4:00 p.m.

clean your mind and clean your shorts

I make it back into the parking lot without falling, but we come to a stop on the edge by the grass and I can't stay upright without my steed's momentum. As I fall, my lance spears the ground and stands like the black obelisk from the movie *2001: A Space Odyssey*. My steed and I collapse at its feet. Sancha stands over us.

"Maybe we'll keep the balancing pole for a while. Maybe get a ten-year-old to show you how to ride a scooter."

I stand up as Sancha is plugging the scooters into an outlet. I jump and let out a whoop in sheer exhilaration from the smooth joy of flying and successfully returning to earth. I turn and look. Atlas is finishing painting something in psychedelic colors over the name of the Laundromat. Now the sign reads: DR. BRAINIAC'S LAUNDROMAT AND BRAIN CENTER. I walk over and read the paper taped to the door:

Clean your mind while you clean your shorts!
Free washer, dryer, and head-shrinker.

The doctor is standing inside the glass door. I open it.

"Your idea, Doctor?"

He shakes his head. "Hers."

Dulcinea has bounced back again. She is painting the walls with brighter colors than I knew existed. And she seems to have more energy than I knew that she had. She is humming a little tuneless song as a sunburst-orange rainbow flows from her fingers across the dingy sky of the neglected wall.

"Hard to say no to her," he says.

"Royalty."

"Royalty."

We stand admiring her for a moment.

"It's good to witness a miracle," I say. "The Bible says, 'Any minor world that breaks apart, falls together again.' I think you've done that for Dulcinea."

He shrugs. "I think Donald Fagan was actually the one who said that. But, no. This is temporary. I gave her a drug that we use in rehab to give people a little bit of a reprieve from the physical effects so we can get them to start the hard work on the underlying causes." He looks at me. "But something was already making a difference with our young queen—DB told me about the way you treat her. Something's elevated her. And it wasn't the sugar."

"Yes, yes. I'm so glad you've cured her. She needs her strength to rule."

"I haven't cured her in a few hours. I've given her a little window. And you and DB have, too. At some point the window will probably close and she'll relapse. They almost always do. The question is what they—and we—do then."

"Yes, yes, of course."

She turns and sees me staring at her with a look of awe. She smiles and gives me a little curtsy.

What a gift! How can I ever find anything wonderful enough to repay her?

day five: 6:00 p.m.

sugar highs and lows

If I can't match Dulcinea's nobility, I can do some small thing for the people in her kingdom. I take a box of the day-old donuts from the counter and walk out to my steed.

Sancha is wiping her steed down with a rag. She looks at me with the donuts in my hand, looks at my steed and my lance, and shakes her head no.

"You're right," I say. "I'll walk. My noble steed deserves a rest."

"Yeah. That's why."

I walk up to 504 Greendale with a box of donuts held out like an offering. I see a man with a dog. I offer him two, for him and his dog. He shakes his head, says donuts aren't good for his dog, so I say, one for now, and one later. He takes them. I walk away, think about it and walk back.

"Wait. You're more careful about what you feed your dog than yourself?"

"You want to run cool, you got to run on any, any fuel. On the other hand, you got to take care of the beings you love, too."

I nod and walk on. Standing at the empty lot at 504 Greendale, I look up and down the street and find the house, where yesterday, the people inside were terrified of me.

I tap, the door opens and a small girl in a lion costume stands before me, hands clawing the air as she roars. I open the box and hold out the donuts, then wonder if I'm spoiling her dinner.

"Maybe half," I say. "Mother? Mama?"

She gives me another roar and claws the air before me in thanks.

The same large man as yesterday is now standing behind the girl. The girl snatches a donut and runs off.

"I . . . not to offend. Sorry yesterday. Brought present."

"You don't have to shout," he says in a surprisingly English accent. "Or wave your hands with every word."

"Sorry, I thought you were . . ."

"Latino? Yes. And English. My father emigrated to England in the fifties. Legally. I do speak Spanish, but I also speak English. Real English."

"Sorry. I just assumed. Donut?"

He steps out onto the small porch and eases the door shut behind him. Takes a donut.

"Don't tell the missus." He eats fast.

"I'm sorry about yesterday." I put out a hand and smile as big as I can. "Don. From the Q."

He wipes sugar off and shakes. "Ingles. My bad, sport. You're not the bad bloke we thought you were. Younger. I think maybe you're his son. Saw you around here a time or two, but we kept our distance."

"We lived here?"

"Maybe your father. I only saw you now and again."

"But my father lived there? You knew my father?"

He swallows. "Nobody knew your father. Always yelling at the kids. Calling everybody on the street 'beaners and mongrels' whether they were Hispanic or Anglo or black. His favorite line the last month or so was to shout, 'I'm going to blow your worthless ass to kingdom come' and then cackle like an old witch. You ask me, he got what he deserved."

"Do you know what happened?"

He stares blankly at the empty lot up the street.

"Did something happen? I didn't see anything."

"Sancha said—"

"Your mate was wrong. Nobody saw anything. In a few days, nobody will be around to remember anything. Anybody on this block who can get out is going. We're moving tomorrow, before ICE shows up and finds a cage for my children. Or worse."

"You said your family emigrated legally?"

"To England. We came over here to visit my brother-in-law, legally, on tourist visas and everything. But he got sick, I went to work to help. That's a crime. Now I'm a wetback

Englishman. Every few months, another neighborhood. Need to stay close, at least until my brother-in-law gets back on his feet."

As he reaches for another donut, the door opens and his wife catches us.

"Nigel! I been working my bloody fingers to the bone to put your dinner on the table and I catch you with a face full of sugar."

"I was just—"

"It was my fault," I say. "He was helping me remember things about my father."

"Your father . . ." She crosses herself and whispers something in Latin. "Ah, that's why you look like him."

Nigel says, "I don't think she ever saw you. At least not with your father." He laughs and pulls his hand back. "If she had seen the way he treated you, she would have raised bloody hell and we'd all be explaining to Fox News why we enjoy living in dog cages."

"No, I'm sure you're exaggerating," I say. "He may have been mean—a little mean—to others. But to his son, to me? No."

"You were there the last time he yelled that he was going to blow us all up. Then he cuffed you one up the side of the head and said, 'and I'm going to blow this one up first.'"

"No, that's just . . . He was obviously teasing. I know my father loved me."

Nigel laughs. "Love? If the nastiness he showed you was love, then I'm—"

His wife grabs a donut and shoves it into his mouth.

"I'm sure he did love you," she says. "Every child deserves to grow up with love. Maybe we just saw a bad side of him."

day five: 8:00 p.m.

stars

Ex nihilo, nihil fit. Out of nothing, comes nothing. How could my father have built an angel in me, when the Ingles say there was so much darkness in himself? Surely, they were wrong.

I wander aimlessly and wind up on the top of Monte Sano, Huntsville's small mountain, at a park centered around a mansion built in the time when Americans enslaved other Americans.

I search my mind for memories that match the Ingles' stories. As usual, I can't find events before my awakening. Just feelings, vague, distant, and hard to identify, let alone understand.

But I can try to put words to those feelings, as a start, even if the start may also be the finish. I take one last look below me. The city lights are just beginning to twinkle, one by one. Maybe I can find a few twinkles inside myself. I close my eyes.

Sadness. The overwhelming emotion I can identify is sadness. But isn't that always the way? Sadness is less an emotion than just a fence around our emotions, or maybe a background color. Shame is here. I can feel myself curling into a little ball, even here in the darkness by myself. Don't hit me. But I don't know who or what I fear. My father? I ask the Ouija board of my subconscious, but there's less of an answer than just the certainty that, whatever I fear, I deserve. Just leave me alone; I can't face what I've created.

There's more. A longing for something; maybe for a world that's never been, or that I was never good enough to see.

Diving into the past is a good phrase. It really is like swimming in the sea. It colors every sense, sucking the warmth out of you and giving it back at times and for reasons that you can neither comprehend nor control. Open your mouth, and the taste will obliterate every other taste. Smell even, although that's also a good way to drown.

And yet you can never really touch it or grasp it.

I realize my weak mind has drifted away from my task. Run away, more like it.

I come back, and see more. A nostalgia, perhaps for something that never existed, but for something warm. Something that feels like Dulcinea's smile, but I know that Dulcinea is the first royalty I've ever met, so it can't be that. But something like it.

And there's something else back there. Something that hurts so much that I can't look at it.

I open my eyes and the sky is full of stars. I look down and see the city below me, a bowl of stars that seem to have fallen from the real stars above and are crying out to return. I walk my eyes across the city, surprised at how many of the stars have stories I can see.

But I can see that there is far more darkness than there is light. That knowledge connects with the feelings I fear, but can only begin to understand. But it also makes the lights brave and beautiful.

Somewhere in the city down there, off to my left, one star is brighter than all the others, calling. I find landmarks, triangulate, and I'm surprised at what I've found.

The Q. Now, with Atlas's lights, my home is the brightest star in the earthly mirror of the heavens, calling to the other paltry earthly lights to shine brighter.

I stand up, back in the present, mind-stepping into the future.

Turn on all the lights. Push back the darkness. Make it brighter.

There is a mission waiting for me.

day five: 10:00 p.m.

tsk-tsk no more

"Time to make it all brighter, Sancha."

As I walk in, Sancha looks up at me from behind the counter, studying her books while customers drop dollars and dimes into the chicken bucket in front of her. She is wearing the darkest sunglasses I'd ever seen.

She taps the glasses. "Man, you let Atlas make it any brighter and not only will I have trouble seeing my laptop, I'll probably get fried sitting here."

The Q is packed. One woman is putting a can of tomatoes on a shelf. I look at her and raise an eyebrow.

"I know you guys are the managers, but it's our store, now. I bought two cans yesterday. Only needed one. Brought the other one back for somebody else."

"Good idea."

"Way we do things here. Another thing I want for my store: think I could put a clipboard at the counter where we could write down stuff that we need ordered?"

Sancha says, "Why not? I've put in three orders today and not had a thing kicked back from the owner. Told you man, the more we lose, the more the owner makes. This way, the community gets a little piece of the American dream, too."

"Yeah, all that sounds good. But, no, Sancha, I don't mean we need more brightness in here, Sancha. Out there."

"Atlas is pumping as much of his artificial sunshine as he can, man. Even with all the light, I don't think you're seeing the truth, man. This was a run-down piece of crap, and you built a community and a clinic and a home and more. You took a little piece of darkness and turned it into the brightness of the Q."

"And there's still too much darkness out there, Sancha. So much darkness, and we just listen to stories about it and go tsk-tsk and let it be."

"Tsk-tsk?"

"Yes. Yes. We've become a nation of tsk-tsk-ers. And we've learned to love it. We hear a horrible story about someone, and we go tsk-tsk and walk away. We love tsk-tsk-ing so much that, when we aren't hearing something to tsk-tsk about, we go to five thousand news sites to read more to tsk-tsk about. And when that's not enough, we go to made-up stories to tsk-tsk about on TV. We are as addicted to tsk-tsk-ing as Dulcinea is to her white powder."

"Maybe we should do a telethon."

"No. If the world were blowing up in an hour, would you do a telethon? You know that story Harriette told us about those women in slavery right around the corner, nobody doing anything but tsk-tsk-ing? The world is blowing up for them, every day. That's a darkness we need to brighten."

"Man, I don't know. If the police can't do nothing, we can't do nothing."

"Of course we can. We are American knights, in the new age of American chivalry. We do things because they are right. And we're doing this."

"Maybe we should talk about it, Don. Maybe get Dr. Brainiac in on it. See if he thinks this is crazy."

"Crazy? Where would America be if George Washington had worried about being crazy before he stood up to the evil king? If the Native Americans had worried about being crazy before they attacked John Wayne with nothing but home-made bows and arrows?"

"Don, listen to yourself. In the first place, Washington didn't really fight a king. Parliament ruled England, even back then. And most of the Natives died fighting the cavalry while John Wayne died in his bed an old man. The brave America you're talking about, that world has already gone the way of knights and chivalry."

"Then at least we won't die tsk-tsk-ing. We will die as noble heroes. Martin Luther King, Lincoln, Superman—Don Q and Sancha. We will die crazy, but proud. And because we're brave, truth and justice and the American way will be on our side."

Sancha studies me for a long time, and I let her make her mind up.

"Die crazy?"

I nod. "Die for something more than tsk-tsk."

There's a long, serious look before she breaks into a crazy smile. "Hell, yeah." She looks at me and laughs. "Thought you were an angel, man, not a hero."

"What is a hero but an angel in action?"

She looks at me with one of those emotions I can't identify. I think about it and realize: admiration. Not sure I've ever seen that before. I like it.

She's pacing.

"But we want stuff, man. Guns and bombs. People. Time. And a plan."

"Can't always get what you want—" She stops me with a look and I shrug without finishing my inspiration. "But we need to strike tonight, or maybe really early, when they don't expect anything."

She seems unconvinced, and I realize I'm losing the admiration.

"Well," I say. "Maybe we do need a plan."

day five: midnight

depends on the job

Dr. Brainiac says, "I think this may be a less than optimal decision."

Sancha has brought Dr. Brainiac and Dulcinea in on our planning. But Sancha describes our mission with less enthusiasm than I expect from her, and the good doctor seems to be picking up on her skepticism.

They're missing the point. "It's not a decision, Doctor. It's a calling. Don't you hear the women crying out for us?"

"Yes. But you can't save everyone, Don."

"Who should we not save in their time of trouble? You? Any of us? Think of what it would mean if everyone knew that, for any injustice, the whole world would always arise, regardless of the risks, just because a fellow human was in trouble. Things like this would never happen. That house of horrors is probably sitting right now in a block of good people, all wanting the women saved. But the bad guys know that the good people can't, or won't, do anything, so they sneer and go about their evil business, even though there are probably a hundred good people for every bad one. But a hundred good people sitting on their butts in safety allows one evil man to rule us all." I look at them, one by one. "And this is not what we are called for in America."

Sancha and the doctor look away. Not Dulcinea. She is sitting on the one remaining washing machine in the old Laundromat, sipping her usual Mountain Dew. Now she jumps down and shakes her finger. "Doctor, didn't you just tell me it's not about regretting your bad decisions, but what you do after?"

"I did. But this is a really, really bad decision."

"How many women in that house would agree with you? I know the answer. Not a one. I know what it means to sit where they are and pray for a savior that will never come."

She looks at me.

"And I know what it means when even one man tries."

Sancha shifts subtly, moving away from the doctor to stand beside Dulcinea.

The doctor looks at us and sighs. "I'm not going to be able to talk you out of this. OK, let's see what we can do to increase the chances of your walking out of there alive."

"With the women."

"With . . . the women. So, what have you got to work with?"

Sancha holds up a roll of duct tape. The doctor arched his eyebrows.

She waves the tape at him. "Worked last time. Now we've got scooters."

"OK. Have you thought about time?"

I hate to discourage ideas, but even I know better. "I don't think time travel really works, Doctor."

"No, I mean, what time are you doing this?"

"Whenever we can get ready."

"Shoot for very early morning, maybe four or five. People's energy and attention are at their lowest point then. Their customers should be gone. Whoever's guarding things may be asleep, or at least inattentive."

"Five a.m. Good."

"And go as dark as you can. Invisible, if possible."

Sancha holds up our black hoodies. "Worked last time."

"Yeah." The doctor scratches his head. "But once you are visible, consider this: If an animal wants to scare a predator, he makes himself look big. Like when a cat bows up or a dog's hair stands on end."

"So you want us invisible but huge?"

Sancha says, "You can't do both."

"Faith, Sancha, faith. My heavenly father says, 'To change the world, you must first change your mind.'"

"That was Jimi Hendrix. And it didn't work out for him, either."

Dulcinea jumps off the washer. "Wait. You *can* change your body."

She runs out the door and comes back with two double-X sized hoodies, and every adult diaper we sell piled in her arms. "Try this."

I worry about what we are going to try with the diapers, but as usual, my Dulcinea is thinking on a plane far above our own. We put the hoodies on and she and the doctor shove diapers into the shoulders, turning us into giants.

Dulcinea beams. "My champion! I want to go with you."

"No," we all say in unison.

Dr. Brainiac says, "I'll keep her with me."

"Please. Keep her and the Q safe until DB and Atlas get back from their half of the mission."

"Wilco. I think I've got the easy part. Don't forget to come back yourself."

"Wilco."

Sancha and I turn and admire our reflections in the plate glass window. I've got to admit that we look pretty terrifying.

"We bad, we bad," says Sancha.

Dr. Brainiac sighs. "Maybe they'll laugh to death."

Sancha pulls up her hood. It is so big it looks like a monk's cowl, completely burying her sweet face into an obscure, non-human form. I pull mine up, too, and stand beside her.

"Not just bad," I say. "We bad-ass."

Dr. Brainiac said, "Bad asses, with no weapons."

"Oh no," I say. "Atlas got us some heroes' weapons."

day six: 4:00 a.m.

lightning bolts from the gods

We sit in the parking lot, balanced on black scooters, sheathed in black costumes in a black, black night. But Sancha and me, we have our own light. Yeah, we have the light, and nothing can stop us from bringing it. Our steeds are fully charged and chomping at the bit; Sancha has our weapons clamped under one arm. Nothing can stop us now.

I nod to her and she twists the power on and rolls like a fearsome and silent shadow in the night. She looks back and slows to wait for me. I raise one invincible gloved fist and twist the throttle.

And fall over sideways at her side.

"Your balance pole, man."

I fetch my lance and try again. Much better.

May in North Alabama is hot, but there is a cool breeze in the lull before the dawn and we sail silent and invisible, just us and a couple of random cars on their way to their own early missions. We get to the last corner before the house and I hold up a fist for Sancha to stop. We study the house. I point to the lone figure on the porch with a cowboy hat pulled down over his eyes.

Sancha nods. She points to her chest and then to a just-blooming dogwood tree in the yard to the left of the hopefully-sleeping man. I nod, and she pulls away, a ghost, almost an imagined thing. As I start to follow, I see headlights flare behind me.

Too late to yell, too late to stop.

I close, the car closes on me. And the man on the porch stirs.

His hat tilts up, he sees the car and something he can't identify caught in the headlights of the car. He stands up, puts his hand on his chair, and squints at us.

Sancha has snuck past him, to the cover of the tree. She reaches under her arm and pulls out one of Atlas's fluorescent light tubes. She rubs it furiously on her sleeve until she awakens a million tiny lightning bolts in the tube.

Cowboy sees the flash, turns, and steps down just as Sancha throws her lightning bolt, a magnificent dark hero illuminated by the sparkles of her own weapon. The tube flickers as it flies, fading until it passes under a power cord and ignites with an angry fire that lights up the entire scene.

I try to squeeze my ears shut against the coming explosion just as the car pulls around me. I realize that we have not tried the tubes to see how big their explosion is. What if the explosion is too powerful? What if the tube blows up the house? We want the cowboy shocked, not dead. What if he has children? What if he's something nice, like a Boy Scout leader, in his spare time? I try to reach out with my lance to stop Sancha's bomb, but it is too far away and it is falling to its victim far too fast.

I flinch as it hits the ground at his feet. The tube makes frail "pop," and the three of us stare at it. The cowboy laughs.

Sancha is trying again, the second bolt flying upward as the car accelerates past us. The cowboy is pulling his gun and Sancha is pinned in the headlights. I twist the throttle hard and push my lance as far forward as I can.

Like a moment destined by God Himself, it all comes together: the pop of Sancha's tube, the blast of the cowboy's gun, and my lance burying itself in his chest at the same moment. I'm knocked off my steed and collapse on the porch on top of him. From nowhere, Sancha runs past, snatching his gun and throwing the roll of tape at me.

"Hold him."

She goes past, into the house, and I see what she means. The poor cowboy is wheezing, in terrible pain. I put my arms around him and try to comfort him.

"You'll be all right. You'll be with your children and the Boy Scouts tomorrow. I'll take care of you."

He's breathing a little better when Sancha comes back out, holding the cowboy's gun and pushing a big black man.

"Do him, too. Wait. What? I told you to hold him."

"I am."

"With the duct tape. Hurry."

I wrap him up and she motions for me to wrap her guy's arms. She pushes him down on the cowboy.

"Now wrap them both together. Get their mouths."

When I'm done, she looks down and laughs.

"Bad guy burrito."

Up the street, there is one glowing headlight. It grows into an old van with one light out, and stops in the yard. Atlas, DB, and a man who looks like Sancha get out.

"Inside," says Sancha. "Hurry."

They come out with a line of terrified young Asian and Hispanic women, each clutching a cardboard suitcase or a pillowcase stuffed with their belongings, each with the dead look of people used to being herded with neither a voice nor an understanding. The last woman is older, maybe a worn-out forty, but looking sixty, holding a girl of perhaps ten by the hand. She drops to her knees in front of Sancha and unleashes a torrent in Spanish. Sancha pulls her up and points her to the van.

"She blessed us for saving her daughter. Said the evil ones were already showing her to customers, getting ready for an auction."

"Couldn't the mother stop that?"

Sancha gives me the pitying look again. "She would probably be retired with a bullet before that happened. Who knows? Maybe the winning bidder would get to pull the trigger."

The van pulls away as sirens begin to scream in the distance.

day six: 5:00 a.m.

the very thin blue line

Sancha drags me into the yard and pulls my scooter out of the dirt.

"C'mon, we gotta go."

I'm straddling my scooter when headlights with blue flashers flare at one end of the street. Then the other.

"Shit," says Sancha. She grabs me by the arm and drags me, and both our scooters, into a clump of untrimmed bushes next door.

"Shit, shit." She dashes out low as headlights sweep the yard, and grabs my lance. Runs back and drops down beside me.

"Sancha, we need to tell them what we've done. The world needs hero stories."

"Keep your hero mouth shut. That's called a confession."

I give in to her. "I don't understand this world."

Cops in blue uniforms spill out onto the porch and stare down at the gift-wrapped men. A new pair of headlights joins the others, and a lone figure gets out.

Harriette. She walks up to the porch slowly and stands looking down at the shattered light bulbs and the duct-taped miscreants while an officer talks to her. She nods and then raises her head like it weighs a hundred pounds. She slowly shuffles her body around in a three-sixty by scuffing her feet like she's too stiff and tired to turn her head or her body. She pauses a micro-second as her eyes go past us.

She says to the officer, "You boys go inside and secure things. I'll look around out here."

"Yes, ma'am. I'll stay out here with these—"

"Take them with you. Inside. All of you. Now."

They disappear and she comes down the steps, pausing with effort on each one and makes her way over to us. When she gets close, I start to stand up, but Sancha snatches me down and clamps a hand over my mouth.

Harriette pulls her phone out and pretends to be talking on it while looking at us. "What the hell have you idiots done now?"

She says some other things but I won't repeat them because she was obviously talking about someone else. And the language was shocking, coming from a lady.

Sancha explains. Harriette appears to grow older as she listens.

"The women. What happened to them?"

Sancha says, "You don't want to know, ma'am."

"If I'm in this, I do."

"Someone is taking them to a small town where he has family. The town has cafes and agricultural plants where they can get jobs and start over."

Harriette mutters more of the words I'm surprised at. She clearly needs me to explain this.

"We saved them. And wrapped up the criminals for you. But we don't want a reward."

Harriette makes a noise and gets a look on her face that makes me think of the line, "Even little old ladies can become killers." I shrink back against Sancha.

"Saved? Those women are probably stopping the car right now so they can run back to the life. And the bail will be waiting for these mooks before we get them to the station. If they even let me take them to the station. If I even have a job after they figure out how to explain this and who to blame."

She turns to look at a pair of headlights coming down the street, lighting a path for an expensive black limousine. The people inside the car see the lights and turn around.

"See that? Customers are already taking their business somewhere else." She stares at the car and I see something in her expression.

I say, "Do you know that car?"

"Yes."

She sighs.

"This fake superhero business has got to stop. Do you know how lucky you were? Bullets don't bounce off of you. You can't leap tall buildings.

You don't even have the power of an insect. This will not end well."

Another sigh. Another of the sad looks directed at me.

"Wait until I get in the doorway, then get out of here. And stop this. You're not helping anybody."

I think of the woman with the child.

"Two people," I say. "Maybe."

Sancha grabs my mouth, hard.

day six: 7:00 a.m.

is that all there is?

We roll back into the Q just as the dawn comes up, the sun and Atlas's renovations fighting to light the world. Atlas and DB run out to meet us.

"Oh man, you're alive," says DB.

I don't understand. "I've been alive all my life."

"No, I mean. You did it!"

Sancha holds her hand up waiting for a high-five.

"We damned well did it."

DB and Sancha complete the high-five and cheer.

DB reports, "Women freed."

Sancha adds, "Bad guys wrapped up. All the good guys, home without a scratch."

More hoots.

Sancha says, "You should have seen our noble knight here, spearing a bad guy like a hero from back in the good old days. Saving the damsels in distress."

They look at me, waiting for glory.

"Maybe," is all I can say. I walk away to the Brainiac Center and leave them to their visions.

Dulcinea and the doctor are sitting in two folding chairs. Dulcinea jumps up, runs over, and hugs me. "You're alive!"

Apparently, after twenty-two years, the whole world has learned this.

The doctor smiles at me but interrupts her. "Thank God you made it. But we're about to start a group session. Join us."

I drag up an orange crate.

He says, "Now everybody sit in a circle."

I'm not sure whether to sit down or not.

"Actually, it's not a circle, Doctor. It's a triangle. If I sit equidistant from both of you it's an equi-lateral triangle. But if I pull back, and put you up a little higher, we can make it an isosceles triangle, showing deference to you as our leader—"

"Just sit down."

I take my seat on the crate, and he turns to Dulcinea.

"You were saying that you feel like there's less of you today, somehow, Dulcinea."

She looks at me with her sad, all-seeing eyes.

"Yeah. I mean, I feel like I'm just slipping away and don't even know what I am—"

"Yes!" I jump up. "Exactly what happened to me last Monday. We are kindred spirits. Doc, do you think we have the same thing, maybe something contagious or some kind of kismet between two linked souls?"

He looks at me sadly. I realize that a lot of people look at me sadly.

"No, Don. I really don't think you and Dulcinea have the same problem."

Dulcinea looks at me for a long time. "I wish I were you. What you did for those women. What you do for me, every time you look at me and make me feel like I'm . . . something. But I'm not you. You gave up yourself and became something more. On my own, I'm nothing."

My heart turns over and I smile at her humility, amazed that I even exist in her world.

"There." She leans forward, searching my face. "How do you do that? Is it a trick? One little twist of your face and I feel so . . . real. There is so much darkness, and all you see is light."

"I am just a poor reflection of you."

She laughs but it's a harsh, hateful laugh.

"I wish. I wish for just one moment I could save someone."

Now I'm ashamed for misleading her. Misleading everyone.

I hang my head. "We didn't save anyone. We strutted and pretended and thought we had pushed a few grains of sand up the hill but they tell me they will all come rolling back. Harriette says this will amount to less than nothing." I paused. "I'm no angel. I'm not even much of a man, and I'm not sure I have any purpose at all."

I look up for her reaction, but Dulcinea has slipped away, her head rolling on her beautiful chest.

"She's fading fast, Don," Dr. Brainiac says. "The sugar and the drugs are fighting the physical addiction, but she has so little strength." She is snoring and snapping her head up for a moment and drifting away again. "But she fights so hard. That little speech of hers—and the speeches she's been giving me about how inspiring you are to her—they cost her a lot. Every voice inside her is telling her to curl up and die, but she's not. And that's one hell of an achievement at this point."

"So how long until she gets her strength back? A day? A week?"

He gives me that sad look again.

"Let's talk about you, Don. From the celebration out there, sounds like you had a pretty good night."

Suddenly I'm crying.

"It's all going wrong. I thought I was an angel. I thought I was rescuing the queen. Now they tell me it was nothing, and you tell me Dulcinea is slipping away. Harriette says that I'm stupid and dangerous. How can that be? It has to make some sense. Why was I placed so carefully at this particular place and this particular time, but given no idea of my meaning or purpose? There has to be a reason."

"Good luck with that. Maybe that's what's going on with you, Don. Maybe you just can't accept a life without purpose, like the rest of us do. Maybe you can't accept everything that you've been told and, like a dog with bad kibble, you've responded by throwing it all up. Maybe it's just chemical, the wrong amino acids." He paused. "Shortly before your . . . event, did you have any surgery that required anesthesia?"

"How would I know?"

"True."

He looks around the room. Surveying his domain, I guess. A load of clothes is spinning in the washer, and the boys and Sancha are singing a very drunk version of "Another One Bites the Dust" in the parking lot.

Probably not the high point of the doctor's career.

"Some of the drugs used for anesthesia are amnesiacs. I've never heard of one of them having an effect like this. But, as a fail-safe, these drugs all have an antidote that can be given if something goes wrong. Maybe we could try an anti-amnesiac."

"Think that would work?"

"Maybe. If you want to risk what's hiding back there."

"Maybe."

Dulcinea opens her eyes and shakes her head.

"No." She turns to the doctor. "Not unless it's safe. We're not going to lose our Don."

"It's not. I'd have to use a high dose to get any effect, and, since we don't know what caused this, we don't know what it would do. Maybe we'd get the old Don. Maybe nothing. Maybe real damage."

"No," she says.

He looks at me.

"You heard the queen," I say.

day 6: 8:00 p.m.

some things motivate you

I go home to my TV to bury myself in real heroes' stories. I sit on the couch, but I can't slip into the role of the Navy SEAL on the screen, or even the slapstick assistant. And if you're not somebody in the story, you're nobody.

Sitting here, I was nobody. Until I saw myself on the screen. Literally, me.

Just when the SEAL is about to reveal the answer to all of our questions, leaving everybody happy (except, of course, the pile of dead bodies at his feet. Maybe their families weren't happy, either. And their baristas and bartenders and, well, you get the point. Those of us sitting on our asses would be happy). Just then, our mayor decides he wants to talk to us. The screen blinks in mid-word for the SEAL, and our beloved mayor's face appears with its usual expression of deep concern for all of us little people who are dependent on his loving, fatherly protection.

Behind him stands Harriette, expressionless, trying her hardest to hide. The mayor shuffles papers on the podium, studies one with an expression of sufficient gravitas, and looks directly into the camera.

"My fellow Huntsvillians. We are under siege tonight."

And that is when I made my television debut. The mayor's face fades and a picture of Sancha and me from last night appears. Sancha is a massive figure in black, floating in the air as she releases a lightning bolt. Another black giant is flying in from the left with a blurry black weapon of some kind, extended. Me. The picture doesn't capture our scooters, so it looks as if we are flying by magic.

"Last night, a Huntsville family was attacked by terrorists with enormous, but still poorly understood, powers. A passing motorist risked his life to capture the only photographic evidence we have. A number of women have been kidnapped for purposes obviously so evil that we can only speculate, and two male citizens were wrapped in a substance that our experts fear might be carcinogenic."

My moment of fame disappears as the mayor reappears.

"We have tasked Detective Harriette Slayer of the Huntsville Police Department to bring these terrorists to justice before anyone else is hurt." He turns to Harriette. "We have made it clear that we will accept nothing less than a quick and total end to this brutal reign of terror. It is your job to bring these probably genetically-engineered monsters in." He pauses. "Dead or alive." He pauses again, waiting for Harriette to acknowledge him, but she just stares straight ahead.

A reporter off-screen takes advantage of the pause to shout, "Mr. Mayor, can you tell us the location of the house, or anything about the house?"

He turns red.

"No. I know nothing about the house. I have never been to that house." He points into the screen. "I. Have. Never. Been. To. That. House."

Another off-screen reporter asks a question about how the mayor's experience as a hero in the last dirty little war is essential in leading the city in this time of trouble. The mayor answers—after sneaking a peek at what appears to be a prepared answer designed to promote his fake heroism.

"We don't need your bluster and pretense," I say, forgetting that the box in front of me was designed to let them deliver messages to me, but not from me to them. "The genetically-modified monster has retired. His lance and his steed are just a two-by-four and a cheap scooter. And he is just a clerk."

The screen flickers again and a very tall man with elegantly-quaffed hair and an expensive suit appears on screen. He is sitting behind a news desk.

"We apologize for interrupting the mayor interrupting your program. We've got a busy night here in the Rocket City. In addition to the mayor's news, WAAT's own Stacey Algood has another frightening story that can't wait."

He looks into the screen with a fixed, worried expression, whispers, "We're off?" and stands to reveal bright purple board shorts under his suit coat. The screen turns to an attractive young woman in a tight dress standing outside a Huntsville night club.

"This is Stacey Algood. We have just learned from a highly-placed government source that the United States government has lost an atomic weapon, and that the weapon is believed to be in the Huntsville area. The highest levels of our government are actively directing an FBI search at this moment to recover the bomb before terrorists detonate it and obliterate all of North Alabama—"

She winces at someone screaming, "Bitch!" behind her. The camera pans as two men in black drag a man with short, perfect white hair into a black pizza delivery vehicle and speed away.

I stand up. I have a mission after all.

day seven: 7:00 a.m.

run while you can

"Get going!"

A blue pickup truck loaded down with all the family's belongings swerves off the road, driving on the sidewalk next to me to try to pass the line of cars flying down my little street. A skinny teen-aged boy sitting in a rocking chair in the truck's bed and holding on for dear life points a bony finger out of town and yells it again.

"Get going, or get blowed up."

I smile and wave at him, and point to the center of the city, where the bomb probably is.

"I'll save us," I yell.

Good to have people encouraging me in my mission.

I dance off into someone's yard as a small, electric car follows the truck and almost gives me a silent death.

"Help is coming," I yell.

Someone else yells "Get going," again.

I try to cross the street to get to the Q, but there is no break in the traffic—both lanes fleeing and traffic rules long gone. I jump onto the back of a pickup, planning to play Frogger from car to car to get across. An old woman leans out of the passenger window and points a gigantic pistol at me.

"Get off."

I yell, "Thank you," and jump on top of an old Volkswagen beetle, bounce to the ground and roll across the grass. I jump up in Rocky pose and yell, "Help is coming." Car horns blare in appreciation.

When I get to the Q, my whole crew is on full alert and ready for action.

"Sancha, glad to see you came in for our mission."

She raises her head off the counter.

"This seems as good a place to die as I've got." There is a pause before she puts her head back down. "God, my life is pathetic. Might as well blow it all up."

"Maybe tomorrow. Today, the world needs heroes, and we're here. You did see the news last night?"

Without raising her head, she waves an arm outside. "Think there's anybody who didn't get the word?"

"Some men run away. Some men run to the sound of the battle."

"Yeah, well, this girl's running to a nap. If I'm going to blow up, I want to do it in my sleep. Leave me alone."

"Sancha, this isn't about us. Maybe it's OK to give up on yourself, let it all just blow up while you dream. But what about all of them out there? It can't be OK to turn your back on them. What if the little girl we rescued just yesterday is back in town, can't get out, and is going to be blown up if we don't save her? And a half million more as well?"

She turns her head sideways in the cradle of her arms. "Leave me alone."

"No. We are heroes. We were sent here to save the world. This is my mission."

"Well, I don't suffer from White Man's Burden like you because A) I'm not white, B) I'm not a man and—most important, C) I know how that turned out before for the little people."

"No! I don't think I'm superior." I pause and consider her words. Is that all my reset is, just savior's ego? "I don't know, Sancha. I'm just a clerk, like you. People give us their pocket change and think nothing of us. The pictures in the papers that make us out to be superheroes—we know that's just adult diapers and light bulbs. We think we are ordinary people who, by a momentary mistake, are heroes. What if we've all got it backward? What if we're all heroes, who, by mistake, think we are ordinary?"

She raises her head. "I'm an ordinary person, who's soon going to be ordinary dust, no matter what she does. So I choose to put my head down."

"Yes! Yes! You are what you choose. Maybe something chose to make me a hero or an angel one day, but I choose it myself now, every day.

With as little strength as I have, with as little time as I have, I choose to be a hero and save the world."

"I think you're a melodramatic delusional." She stands up. "But someone's got to keep you out of trouble. So what exactly does this bomb of yours look like?"

day seven: 8:00 a.m.

stop the bleeding first

There is a force for good in the universe, and I am one of its hands. If I just give myself to that goodness, it will give me the tools I need to make the world better. As proof of this, another gift appears at this very moment. The TV that had been showing highlights of a Rocket City Trash Pandas baseball game, blinks and shows Vice President Bob Pilgrim standing before a podium, with his name and very important title below him, flanked by grim-looking men in dark suits.

"There is grave danger to the citizens of Hunts-ville . . ." One of the men whispers in his ear. ". . . and North Alabama . . .," the man whispers again and Pilgrim says, "Really, do we need to cover that much?" The man nods and Pilgrim exhales. "I come before you to tell you not to panic. There was a rumor circulated from a bar last night—" He hesitates. "A bar that I was not at. A rumor that your government has . . . misplaced a device of some sort. No one knows or can verify the source of that rumor." He glares at the camera for that. "And I can neither confirm or deny whether the missing device is, in fact, an atomic weapon."

"That's comforting," I say. "Maybe it's not that bad."

"Yeah," says Sancha.

Pilgrim looks into the camera gravely. "But I would like to point out two things: a member of our government at my level would not be here if it was not safe, nor would a member of your government with my authority be here if we were not doing everything possible to secure this device as soon as possible." He pauses. "Whatever this device is. I would like to encourage you to have confidence in the future our beloved president is bringing you, and not to listen to rumors in bars."

Sancha says, "Really comforting. I don't think he could find his ass without a drink in his hand. And I believe rumors in bars more than I believe him."

I look at her and nod. Sancha's smart.

As he turns to leave the podium, a voice calls out, "Sir, can you tell us the size of the bomb?"

He starts to turn away, then turns back with a smirk and an answer.

"If it is a bomb, it is tiny. Minuscule, really. Tiny. I can confirm that this is physically the smallest nuclear weapon in the American inventory."

Sancha says, "Still comforted?"

"Maybe not."

She opens her computer and goes to work.

I go to tell the guys in the Brainiac Center of our mission and assure them that we are on the case. But, a crash behind me tells me we have other things to worry about. I spin around.

A delivery van has smashed into a pickup truck, both loaded with as many people as they can hold. Now those people are reduced to a carpet of moaning bodies with red blooming from within like a movie special effect.

But this is real. I run to a man with a small red fountain gushing from his upper leg and press hard to stop the bleeding.

"Femoral artery," I yell. "Tourniquet, now. Get me gauze." I strip out my belt and wrap it as tight and as fast as I can.

My crew appears around me, like miracles called by my prayer. They each grab a red river somewhere around me. Dr. Brainiac has one hand on a bleeding arm and raises it up as high as he can while maintaining pressure and surveying the scene.

"No, DB," he says. "Leave him. That one will be all right on his own. Take that woman, there. Someone take . . ." He looks around and sees that he has no more resources. His man is moaning and waking up. Brainiac grabs the man's good hand and clamps it onto the wound. "Hold that."

He runs into the Q and comes out carrying every kind of tape and cloth he can hold. He drops them on the ground beside me and tears the packaging away from a pair of scissors. He bends down beside the man I'm working on and starts cutting the man's pants leg, both of us working together to keep the blood stilled.

"You've done this before," he says.

"Maybe. The color of his leg still looks good."

"Yeah. Maybe a puncture and not a tear. May have a chance. Let's get pressure and move on, get back to him when we've got everybody stable."

We work furiously until we have a feminine hygiene pad strapped to him with my belt. I tighten the belt and stand up.

"Seems to be holding," he says. "Let's check him every five minutes. A femoral artery puncture's dangerous, even in the OR, but he's got a chance."

He surveys the crowd. A woman and a man are standing up, shaking themselves back to life.

"Take that one," he points to a woman on the fringe soaked in red and I run to her. I hear him directing the new man and woman where to join in the fight, then check on the others.

Sancha comes running out and gets to me as I fall on my knees beside the bleeding woman. Not as bad as it looked; her blood is coming from a number of superficial wounds, already slowing. I bend down to check her pulse and breathing.

Sancha says, "Where do you want me?"

"Back inside. Try to find out if the hospital is still open, if ambulances are running." The woman's breathing is good, her pulse strong. "And try to stay on the bomb, too. We've still got to save the world."

I look around. This is not my mission, but here we are.

"After we do this. Go."

She runs back inside.

There is a baby crying somewhere and I pick my way over and carefully check the baby. No visible broken bones, and his lungs are obviously working. The woman beside him must have wrapped herself around him and kept him alive. I know he shouldn't be my priority, but I pick him up anyway. I look for someone to take him and I see Dulcinea coming toward me. I go to hand her the baby.

She stumbles, just a little. Her eyes are dilated, and she is smiling a vacant smile. Smiling in the middle of all this.

She holds out her arms. "I've got to help."

I look into her magic eyes, crazy today. Maybe Sancha and the doctor are right and someone is feeding my queen something that is not good for her. There is still royalty in her somewhere, but she's gotten hold of a hit somehow and the monster has her today.

But she has her arms out. Her arms need filling as much as we need the help.

I pull the baby back.

"Go in the Q. Grab all the first aid supplies and rubbing alcohol you can find, and bring them out to the doctor."

Still smiling, she turns, tries to skip, slips and laughs, but makes it back inside. I tuck the baby under one arm and go to where Dr. Brainiac is calling me.

day seven: 7:00 p.m.

picture perfect

Sancha somehow rounds up enough ambulances to get the worst cases to the hospital, where doctors and nurses are remarkably still working. I sit down just as the two government workers come back in for more coffee. I look at them in their crisp business suits and wonder if they are the only people left in Huntsville without blood on their hands. The tall one—Zhong is her name—shrugs.

I point her to the coffee machine. "You'll have to make the coffee yourself. We've been kind of busy."

"Believe it or not, we have, too."

"Must be some important work you're doing."

She pauses. "While I can neither confirm or deny the nature of our business—yes. Yes, it may be the most important work in the world right now. Certainly, the most important work here in Huntsville—if we can get through the agency BS and get it done." She looks out the window at the crowd gathering in the parking lot, people who can't get out but are coming here for whatever help we can give them.

Dr. Brainiac has a couple of the walking wounded next door, doing what he can with anyone who can wait to go to the hospital. He and DB have Dulcinea helping them, mostly so they can keep an eye on her, but she is helping as much as she can. The Q itself is packed with the semi-able bodies. We picked up a load of corn at the market yesterday (yesterday? It seems as far away as the land before my awakening), and Atlas has a fire and a pot set up in the parking lot, handing out ears of boiled corn as fast as he can.

"Looks like you've got your own work here," Zhong says.

I wave it away. "This isn't my real work. I, too, have important work, once I get this settled, and Sancha comes back from getting something we need for our mission. Meanwhile, maybe coffee will fuel your quest. We've got some better coffee today."

"I doubt if our boys will notice. We'll make ours, leave you the money, and fill up the pots for you. Looks like you can use it, too."

I realize that I am bone-tired. The sun is going down and I feel as ashamed as the darkness when I realize I have wasted a day that my hero's mission desperately needs.

"Thanks. I'll take a cup. A big cup."

They hand me a big cup from the first batch and I take it over to the Brainiac Center to drink it while I check on things there. Brainiac stares at it like a hungry puppy and I hand my coffee over to him.

"I think we're stable," he says after the first big gulp. "For now. Maybe. I just sent a pickup full of the worst over to the hospital. Hospital says they'll stay open as long as they can."

"We have to do that, too."

He nods.

I look in the corner. Dulcinea is sleeping, or maybe passed out, with three kids snuggled up on her. DB is at my shoulder.

"I finally got her to sleep," he says to Brainiac. "Told her the kids needed her body heat."

"She kept trying to help," says Brainiac. "But she can't focus. Was doing more harm than good. Every time we tried to get her to rest, maybe sleep off some of the dose she got so we can start over, she'd pop back up, saying, 'Don needs my help.'"

"When we find the bomb," I said. "And restore order and get back to normal—after all that, what can we do with her now that she's high again?"

"Start over. Find where she got whatever she got. Stop it from happening again. Rehab's tough. Nobody ever succeeds without backsliding. But she's trying, and that's the hard part."

DB looks hurt. "Man, I'm doing my best, too. I watch her every minute, but then this happens. I don't know. Maybe her connection came by and I missed him. Maybe, maybe. Sometimes this stuff seems to fall from the sky like a poison rain."

Brainiac says, "Didn't mean to sound like I was blaming you. I know you can't do it all. Much as we can help, Dulcinea's got to do it herself. And she's got to get stronger, in every way."

I say, "We have to find something to remind her that she's a queen."

"Why the hell not?" DB says. "None of the other crap works."

I go back next door and Zhong hands me another cup as I walk in. Sancha comes behind me and Chavez dances over to her with a big smile and holds the door for her. Sancha smiles back and I think of Dulcinea's smile earlier. Dulcinea's smile meant she was lost to the world; these girls' smiles mean they are lost in each other and still finding some beauty in each other, even in the worst of the world. I wonder what it means that we use the same expression "lost to the world" for such different things. I shake myself back as I realize that I need to focus.

Sancha is saying, "Turning nasty out there. Gangs everywhere. Saw a bunch of pre-teen girls dragging automatic weapons out of a pawn shop. Teen-aged boys carrying a big TV. TV? What the hell they think they're going to do with that? Watch porn while the world blows up around them?"

Chavez pushes one of Sancha's papers at Zhong.

"Look at this."

Sancha says, "Yeah, I figure it's the only place to start. Maybe if we put up flyers, somebody'll remember seeing something and give us a starting point. Went to the library, only places open now are libraries and hospitals, wouldn't you know. Librarian found a way to get an internet connection, and we looked up the smallest bomb in the US arsenal and printed a hundred copies."

I peek around Zhong. The words on the flyer read HAVE YOU SEEN THIS BOMB? TELL THE Q, and gives the address and the cell numbers of everybody here. Below is a diagram of a bullet-looking thing about the size of a child with a serial number underneath.

Sancha says, "That's what the bomb looks like."

Zhong and Chavez exchange cryptic looks. Zhong hands it back to Sancha.

"Sounds like as good an approach as any. Call us if you hear anything."

Chavez looks at Sancha. "Mind if we take a few? Put them up where we work?"

day seven: 8:00 p.m.

the gift of the magi

Sancha and I stand in the doorway, and watch Chavez and Zhong leave with their coffee as more families drift into the parking lot. The random gunfire throughout my city makes it seem like we're inside a big, dark popcorn popper.

"OK, Sancha. What's next? Put up flyers?"

She studies the side of my face and listens to the popping outside.

"Tomorrow morning, man. You need rest, not a bullet."

"The city needs help more than I need sleep."

"Hold your hands out."

She pushes my hands and I try to push back but I've got nothing.

She drops her hands. "The city needs a hero, not a weak kitten. Get some food, get some sleep. Save the world at daylight."

She walks away and an old man walks up, trying to smile. "Mister, can you tell me where a boy might find a bed?"

I grinned, shook my head. "No," was all I said. But then I added, "I can, however, offer you a square of our finest concrete. Would you like king-sized or a double?"

He smiles. "With the right heart, a worn-out dump can become a palace."

"When did you last eat?"

"Sometime back before the world was exploding."

I hand him a Gatorade and a hot dog from Atlas's Bonfire Cafe and point him to an open space behind the counter.

Sancha shakes a finger at me. "You're not going to get any rest here. Go home. Carefully. Rest and come back at first light." She hands me a carton of milk and a ragged doughnut and pushes me in the direction of home.

I pick my way carefully, but things are quiet here. One advantage of living in a poor neighborhood is that there's nothing to steal and little to burn. The pop-pop of the guns sounds far away and unreal. I get inside my house and reflexively turn on the TV. To my surprise, it comes on. I collapse into my chair.

People are running around like crazy in a running gun battle, and I try to figure out what part of town this is and whether anyone is being hurt. I see the Empire State Building and hear theme music and realize that this is entertainment. I see that, although everyone is firing Tommy guns and revolvers that seem to hold hundreds of bullets, there is no blood. One of the actors is a comedian and the music is light.

Ah, a comedy. That means I should be laughing.

I wonder if I lost my sense of humor when I became an angel, or if I need to supply a laugh track for my exploding city.

I go to bed and try to sleep. I discover that the four hundred cups of coffee I had today have done a good job of getting me through the day but are doing a bad job of getting me through the night. Instead of sleeping like I need to, I feel like I'm tied to my bed with my eyes nailed open being tortured for something I don't understand. Tortured for something beyond my understanding or power to change. I identify that feeling as shame. I'm ashamed of something. What?

This answer, though, is as clear as it is painful. My city, my people, my world are all in desperate need. I was sent to save them, but I've done nothing. I've been given tools. I have a steed and a lance, a trusty companion and a palace. And I've done nothing. The fault, dear Brutus, lies not in our tools, but in ourselves.

Courage. Like the cowardly lion, I shake because I don't believe that I have the courage I need. And like the lion, I need to stand up. How do you grow courage? Not by cowering in a bed or accepting the slapstick anesthetic the world wants to pump into me from the TV box. As the dawn starts to show, I get out of bed. I must face a fear in order to grow the courage I need. I see a glow calling to me, a small monster to be slain to prove myself. I go to it. It is the small door in the kitchen. I pull it open, easy this time.

The glow is just a bare bulb hanging from the basement ceiling, left on by Sancha. An ordinary mistake.

But I know a calling when I see one. I must descend into this pit, face my fears, and build the courage I will need for the day.

Step by trembling step, I approach my destiny. At the bottom, I make a slow three-hundred-sixty-degree turn, searching for my worthy foe. There is nothing here but the wall of cardboard boxes that Sancha already found.

Maybe the monster is behind them. I take down the first box. It is empty. I set it aside. The second box is also empty, and the third. All of them. At the bottom is a small metal hat box of a silvery metal I have never seen. I lift the lid and a fantastic light spills out, almost liquid in its texture. Inside is a necklace, glowing with a shimmering light that shifts colors as though from its own will. There are eight beads with different symbols on their faces in the center of the necklace. They spell out, "^o^USA30." It seems like a puzzle in need of completion. I twist the first bead to spell, "Go^USA30." The necklace flashes thirty quick times in appreciation, and then starts a slow throbbing. I finally got something right.

I close the cover and tuck the case under my arm, and fly up the stairs toward the blooming dawn.

This life is like that: you search for what you think you want for yourself, and get a miracle that you need to help someone else—and you are so much richer for it. In searching for courage to strengthen myself, I have found the magical present that I need to show Dulcinea, noble queen that she is.

day eight: 6:00 a.m.

the finest, at their best

In the FBI command center, an alarm like a World War II klaxon sounds: whoop, whoop, whoop. Bells clang, and the device locator screen flashes red. Chavez and Zhong, the only two awake in the center at dawn, watch the room come alive; some agents slowly rubbing sleep from their eyes, others leaping up, weapons drawn, ready for action. By the time they find the source of the alert, Zhong is standing at the display, studying the source. As their eyes slowly focus on the display, she announces, "Gentlemen, we have a hit."

One man cringes and wraps his arms around his head.

"No, Bannon," she says. "Not a detonation." He unwraps his arms sheepishly. "A hit means that the device has been exposed. The good news is that we now have a place to start looking. The bad news is that whoever has opened the case may be in the process of detonating the bomb. We have work to do, fast. And please holster your weapons if you're going to flail around like that."

She punches a button on the screen.

"I've sent the alert. The battle wagons will be manned and warmed up with the coordinates loaded by the time we get to them. Egress to your assigned transport ASAP. You'll receive your orders en route. Go!"

Chavez holds the door and the men run toward it. They stop as Pilgrim blocks them, rubbing a pair of red-rimmed eyes and wearing a Margaritaville pajama top with no bottom. His eyes flutter to full attention when he sees the flashing screen.

"Ready the airborne command center!" he yells. A young woman, wearing the matching pajama bottoms, but no top, appears in the doorway behind him.

Zhong says, "Done, sir. Your plane is revving up and transport is waiting for you and your . . . advisor."

"Good. It's important for you men . . ." he smiles at Zhong ". . . and girls to have confidence that your commander will be available even if the bomb goes boom."

"Yes, sir."

He points at the man who had covered his head.

"Bannon, you're in command on the ground."

He and the young woman disappear. Bannon looks around at the blank faces staring at him.

"What she said."

They all hit the door at the same time. They get stuck, but eventually they all get through.

day eight: 7:00 a.m.

a gift for beauty

Whatever upper or downer or sideways booster Dulce had taken earlier is wearing off and Dr. Brainiac's drugs and all the Mountain Dew in Q-ville aren't helping her much. She sits on the cold concrete before me and won't even look at the box in my hands.

"No presents," is the only sound coming out of the mass of flaming red hair buried in her arms.

"For my queen." I start to open the lid, but a pale, skinny arm shoots out with surprising quickness and slaps it shut.

"No."

It's a simple word but, for the first time, it has the sound of a royal command.

"I am no queen, Don. I am not even much of a woman now. Certainly not to you."

"My queen, you are not seeing clearly. Through my eyes, you are the most beautiful, magical, royal creature there is, or there ever could be. You bring the beauty to the world."

She raises her head sadly and looks at me.

"What happened to you, Don? Did you sleep in a tanning bed or something? You're tanned and, I don't know, glowing today."

People always notice skin-deep changes on the outside, and never the large changes of the heart.

"No, I am still the same servant in awe of his queen."

She looks at me like a small dreamy kid might, whose parents are still telling her about Santa Claus even when she knows better. Knows better, but still needs to believe.

"All you men think every woman brings the beauty to the world."

"No. I mean, yes, I guess that's true. But you have a kindness and sweetness beyond even that."

"Men think all women have that, too. You're wrong about me. At my best, Don, I was a slightly below average woman: too skinny, too . . . lost. I always wanted . . . something, but everybody told me I was too stupid to get it. I always wanted to give something wonderful to the world, but everybody told me I had nothing to give. Or at least, nothing to be proud of. Lots of cheapness to give, favors given in exchange for survival, things given and treated with contempt. You don't know, Don. You can't imagine the things I've done. Nothing you see here is real: not the crown you imagine, not the fantasy life you construct for me. Nothing. Even my hair color—the only thing I like about me—isn't real."

"No, my queen, you're not . . ." I pause. "Maybe. But maybe not, too, at the same time.

Like two visions of one thing. Ignore that you are physically beautiful—"

"—Emaciated. Dirty."

"But that's not the vision that's important. Look at your spirit. It took me a long time to see the struggles that even a queen has. And it makes me admire you more. Who else could fight the battles you fight? Demons within, demons without—and you, rising above it all, a queen. Royalty. Beauty, in a quest that even you don't know if you will win. And that is why, to me, you will always be a queen. The fact that you are willing to wrestle with your demons and get dirty and beat-up, actually give up the flesh from your bones, and still fight back with nothing but a cup of cheap soda—that's what makes you royalty."

I take her hands, and she lets me. As I touch her, her strength flows through our hands into me, as if the connection of our hands is stronger than years of mere talk could ever have forged.

"It's not that I see less, my Dulcinea. It's that I see more. I don't know how, but I do. Not only do I see every filthy thing the world has ever done, years of ugliness and pain and betrayal; men screaming in their death, women crying, children—oh! I won't describe it to your tender heart—but somehow the same soul that cannot remember what it had for breakfast seven days ago now knows all of the pain and evil there has ever been in the world and knows that I used to walk through it trying to find ways to hide. No more."

I stare into her eyes and try not to fall helplessly into those dark blue skies.

"And I opened my eyes on that first day and saw a kindred spirit, doing anything she could to shut out the pain and avoid facing the very hard truth that she was sent here, like me, on a mission that may even be secret to her, but one she is called to and worthy of. And I know you feel there is so little of you left that you fear there is nothing. But the tiny flicker of the nobility left in you keeps demanding that you struggle. And that is your beauty, my Dulcinea. Not Hollywood-whistling beauty, but real beauty. That flaming mop of hair shines like the torch on the Statue of Liberty, made real and walking among us. Who chose it, Dulcinea? Who made it happen, gave it to all of us and asked for not a thing in return? You. Not the woman of chance who was given a name and a certain hair color at birth, and then a lifetime of pain, but the woman of choice who turned it all into royalty and one tiny desperate glimmer of her mission, fighting like a beautiful flower pushing its way through the dirt. You, my queen. You."

I can see she's fading, eyes struggling to stay open. But struggling. I stare into them, unguarded, and let myself see into her. There are tiny specks of light in the twilight of her eyes.

"You have stars in your eyes, Dulcinea. Stars. I think I was made for you."

I'm suddenly embarrassed, and afraid that I've said too much. I release those wondrous hands and look away.

"You don't have to be born in a palace, Dulcinea, to be a queen. Please, accept my humble present. It is only a small token, made by men, but it is there to remind you that anything made by men in this world pales in comparison to the choices of one beautiful queen. And to remind you that one man is certain of that."

She reaches out her hand and rests it on her magic present. But she smiles. Her lips are crooked and cracked, but she smiles.

And then she falls asleep.

day eight: 7:00 a.m.

another one bites the dust

"Don't you people know how to demolish a house quietly?"

Bannon puts a hand over his cell and yells at the team of agents sitting with their laptops at folding tables in the street, supervising, as technicians search Don's house piece by piece. As each piece is removed, it is run through a scanner, cataloged, shrink-wrapped, and carefully stored in its assigned location in the evidence trailers that will be sealed and taken to a secret location.

He puts his hand over his ear and curses the primitive, noisy state-of-the art FBI process of dismantling houses. Surely a billion dollars could be found to make the process quiet and less distracting so he could talk on the phone while they work.

"Yes, sir," he says into his secure cell. "The initial scan found nothing. We believe the device has been removed to an unknown location. Based on the time since detection, we believe the device is in a . . ." He consults the screen in front of him. ". . . a seven-point-six-kilometer circle." He squints at the display, which contains a number of alternate estimates, assuming the device was being moved in a fast car or a Concorde supersonic airliner, which has been out of service for at least ten years, and could not possibly have landed on the street here even when it was in operation. But the FBI covers all its bases.

However, the FBI also values crispness. He starts to add, "Or maybe it's a lot farther away," but decides against that.

Pilgrim's voice says, "How long will it take us to dismantle every building within that radius?"

"We—that is, our technical advisors—don't believe that could be done before the circle could grow uncontrollably large. They did point out that, if Congress had authorized a thousand of these mobile exam teams, as we requested, it might be feasible."

"Damned Congress."

"Yes, sir. The PR team also advised that they probably could not keep that out of the papers."

"Damned press. Why do we have to do everything by ourselves? Maybe we could just blow all of them up."

"Yes, sir."

There was a long pause.

"Maybe that's it. Could the air force take out the whole circle, and ensure that we got the bomb? Quietly, if possible."

"Destroy the city to save it? We've discussed that—are still discussing it. The flyboys have a bomber turning on the runway with a bomb that they swear will do the job."

"Is that the MOAB, the Mother of All Bombs that I heard about?"

"No, sir. This one is much bigger, called the MFOAB. They've been waiting for us to declare war against a small country so they can test it, but now they want to use it on this."

"So what's the holdup?"

"The scientists, sir. They say it will spread radiation from the device, if not set it off."

"Keep the option on the table. Nobody believes scientists anymore. What else?"

A small man in a gray Armani suit tugs at Bannon's sleeve. Bannon yanks the sleeve away.

"Can't you see I'm on the phone?"

"Yes, sir. But I thought you'd want to know. We've identified the owner of the house."

Pilgrim overhears this. "Let's hear it, son."

"It's Donald Becker, sir."

Pilgrim and Bannon inhale simultaneously.

"Not that Donald Becker, sir."

They exhale in unison. "This one seems to work at the Quick Stop convenience center around the corner."

Chavez and Zhong, sitting at the table next to Bannon, keep their heads down but exchange looks across their laptops.

"Pick him up. Hold the bombers until we see what he's got."

day eight: noon

the camera does not lie

I smile at the two men.

"The walls in here are such a strong shade of gray."

They have very politely introduced themselves as FBI interrogators. The one in front has been smiling constantly, and mirrors my every gesture. The one in back always scowls.

Without breaking his smile, Smiler says, "Why thank you, sir. I agree with you."

I look around the room. A precise ten-by-ten square with a large mirror on one wall, a single glaring light fixture in the center, and a couple of tiny red lights ominously flashing in the corner. Three metal chairs. A perfectly square stainless-steel table with a big metal ring.

I am handcuffed to the ring.

"This is such a well-done room," I say. "A place for everything, and everything perfectly in its place. You could decorate my home."

"Why thank you, sir. The FBI prides itself on its efficiency."

"And competence. How do you get the wall color so uniform? We've got cement block walls like this at the Q. There are always little spots and holes in the paint because it's so hard to get paint into all the little indentations in the walls."

Smiler pulls out a tastefully small, leather notebook.

"I'll make a note for someone to call you when we're through, sir, to discuss painting techniques."

"Thank you. That would be so helpful."

"The FBI prides itself on being helpful, sir."

Smiler arranges his hands just like mine. Except for the handcuffs. Scowler pulls the other chair behind him and to the side, so that he is constantly scowling at me over Smiler's shoulder.

"Mr. Becker, we need your help, sir. Do you know anything about the missing nuclear device?"

"Yes, sir. We know everything about it."

"You do?"

"Of course. This is our mission, and we do our homework. You know, you can't count on the same people who lost the device to find it."

Smiler's smile falls a little. "We did not lose . . ." And then the smile comes back. "If you know everything about the device, can you tell us where it is right now?"

I laugh and Smiler joins me, but with some difficulty.

"I'm not superman, no matter what people think. No, we're putting up flyers with a picture of the bomb and asking the whole city to help us. One angel can't do much, but one angel and an energized congregation can move mountains. Or find bombs."

"The city seems to have other interests now."

"Most of them probably haven't seen our flyer."

Smiler nods, adding a touch of graveness to his look.

"We picked up a copy of your flyer, sir." He turns and Scowler puts it into his hands.

"Is this the device, sir?"

"Absolutely. I told you, we're on top of this."

Smiler and Scowler exchange looks. Scowler leans forward.

"This is a picture of the device?"

"Yes, sir. You can keep the flyer. It has my phone number at the Q, if you find it."

"Why, thank you, sir." Smiler turns to Scowler. "I believe it's your turn now."

He stands up, steps aside, and Scowler bulls to the front and stands with his hands on the desk, staring down at me. I move my hands, but he doesn't move with me.

"Why are you lying?"

"I'm not lying. I can't lie; I'm an angel."

"Is that so? An angel with an atomic bomb? Quite a combination, wouldn't you say?"

I smile. It's always good to smile. "Ah, I see our misunderstanding. I don't have the bomb yet. And when I find it, I will return it to its owner. What would an angel need with a bomb?"

"So you haven't seen the bomb? Not at, say, your house this morning?"

My eyes get big.

"No. I left my house very early this morning. You're saying the bomb is there? Did someone get one of the flyers, find the bomb, and put it on my porch after I left? Why are we waiting here? I don't think you recognize the seriousness of this. Gentlemen, let's go."

I rattle my handcuffs, but they don't give.

Scowler turns the chair around and sits down, deepening the scowl to contempt.

"You'd like that, wouldn't you? Lead us on a wild goose chase to your house. Maybe have a few of your militia waiting for us, kill a few God-fearing American agents, maybe cut off our scalps?"

"No, I wouldn't." I pause. "How do you cut off a scalp anyway? Is there a tool? Is this one of those skills that I forgot when I became an angel?"

"Enough of this crap. You're no angel. You're a Becker."

He reaches back and Smiler (who is no longer smiling) hands him a folder.

"Donald Becker."

"I prefer Don. Sancha has started calling me Don Q. Either one is friendlier than—"

"Not you. Donald Becker, Senior. Your father. Head of the America First Militia. America's number one hater. Hates everybody. Hates blacks, Jews, women, children, Catholics, Protestants, liberals, writers, singers, professional athletes who sit down, actors who stand up, you name it. The

Bureau has lost track of him in the last few years, but not his organization."

He leans over, puts his face in mine.

"The organization that secretly infiltrated the government and stole the device."

My jaw flies open.

"You're saying this . . . this man is my father. No. My father is in heaven, waiting to call me home when I've completed the mission he sent me here to do."

"We both know you've been doing missions for your father for years."

I brighten.

"You know some of my earlier missions? I'd love to hear about—"

"Your real father. You've been his errand boy since you were twelve. We've got enough on his militia now to bury all of you for a hundred years, either in a cesspool here or in a third-world torture prison of our choosing."

"No, you don't understand. Maybe this man was my contact here. Maybe you misunderstand the things we've done."

Scowler opens the folder with a sigh and spreads three photos on the table in front of me.

"These are so disgusting, even I can't look at them for long."

I recoil, but the handcuffs hold me like a dog on a chain, just as the photos hold my eyes with their horror. My mouth keeps saying, "No, no," but I can't look away. "No one can hate that much."

"Your dad, and you, can. I'm always amazed at how easy it is for human beings to hate, but you and your father go beyond anything I've ever seen or heard about." He leans into my face. "And, from what we hear from his members—" He pauses. "—from his other members—is that he has decided to hate white people, too, for letting things get to this point. So now he hates everybody. And he's got a son who does anything he wants."

Emotions race over me like summer thunderstorms. I fight them back, and return to my smile. I turn the pictures face-down and shove them away.

"Thank you for your good work on behalf of our country, agent. But you're simply mistaken. I cannot be that Donald. If you notice, despite their horror, none of those pictures show me. Now, if you'll release me, I have important work to do, fighting these very forces."

Scowler shoves one last photo across, with as much tenderness as his scowl permits.

I flinch. On first look, it is a picture of a lynching, a black man and a white woman hanging from a tree. There is a small crowd of men covered in hoods and robes standing by. Between the men and the victims stands a man, unmasked, gazing at the bodies with pride and—there is no other word for it—lust.

Next to him stands a boy in his young teens. The boy is staring up at the man with admiration and pleading. Both the boy and the man look a lot like me.

The two agents walk out of the room and leave me to stare at the photo.

day eight: 2:00 p.m.

even girls can do this

Smiler and Scowler walk into the command center briefing room. Except Smiler is now scowling and Scowler now wears a worried look.

Pilgrim is at the podium.

"Ah, the experts."

Smiler pauses. "I thought you were in the command center, sir."

"The President tweeted that I should return here."

"Ah…Welcome back?"

Pilgrim growls and picks up his drink and takes a seat in the audience. Smiler, scowling, mounts the platform with the gravitas of a man giving a eulogy at a state funeral. There is a hand waving furiously in the audience.

Smiler says, "Yes, sir."

The man stands at attention.

"If the bomb was at the site we searched yesterday, but it's not there now, then someone is moving it. Do you experts know if the device can be detonated by shaking?"

"We're not that kind of experts."

Smiler pauses and waits for the bomb expert to stand up. No one stands up.

Pilgrim says, "Don't we have an explosives expert on this team?"

One man stands up. "We do, sir, but every expert on this device insists on staying in a secret bunker underground. Far underground. Far away."

Pilgrim mutters a curse. "Well, check the damned manual."

Nobody volunteers.

"You mean nobody has the manual?"

Again, no volunteers.

"Idiots."

He waves for Smiler to continue. Smiler clicks the remote and the big screen is filled with a frozen image of Don in the interrogation room. One side of the screen has glowing red abbreviations like CRED and EVAS. He hits play and Don starts cheerfully explaining that he is the angel who will find the bomb. Numbers appear next to the labels, going up and down. The numbers are generally green, occasionally changing to yellow as the numbers dip. Smiler pauses the interrogation when Don is excited to go get the bomb with the FBI men.

Someone in the crowd laughs. "He's an idiot."

Smiler points to a label: INT.

"That's the IQ imputed by the analysis software. He's 165, probably higher than any man in this room. But that's not what's important.

Look at the near-perfect numbers for CRED throughout."

Pilgrim says, "Good for him. Where's the device? I need to get back to Washington. You promised you would get that out of him."

"That's the problem, sir. He honestly doesn't know."

"You mean he honestly thinks he's an angel?"

Smiler squirms. "Yes, sir. But there is this, sir." He runs the video forward, pauses with Don looking at the picture of the father and the son. "Look at these numbers, sir. His credibility is still high, but his stress level is through the roof."

"Meaning what?"

"I don't know, sir."

"Idiots. I give you one job, ask where the device is, and you can't do it."

Smiler hangs his head.

"So what do we do with him? Elimination? Bury him in a foreign prison?"

"I honestly don't think he's a threat, sir."

"We're not going to send him back to his convenience store, although that might be punishment enough. Have you seen the wines they carry in those places?"

"That may be exactly the right approach, sir. While we don't think he can lead us to the device, there is something going on between he and his father. Perhaps if we release him, and have a team follow him, we can be there if his father tries to contact him."

"All right." Pilgrim turns to Bannon, who he is now treating as second-in-command since he put Bannon in charge of the search yesterday. "Who have we got available?"

"No one, sir. Every man already has an important assignment."

Pilgrim points at Cheech and Chong.

"What about them?"

The two women maintain the impassive professional look they've learned to use to respond to idiotic ideas.

Someone in the back says, "Yeah. Let the angels help the angel find the device."

Laughter.

The same guy says, "Can they still get coffee?"

Pilgrim stands up. "Why not? Women always say they can do twice as much work as men."

Lots of laughter.

And some people say the bureau has no sense of humor.

day eight: 8:00 p.m.

riders on the storm

I say, "You guys sure drink a lot of coffee. Is that all your government agency does? Drink coffee? Even at . . ." I look at the clock on the wall that Atlas now has working. ". . . eight o'clock at night?"

Chong says, "Pretty much."

"You did hear that the world, at least locally, may be coming to an end unless someone does something?"

"Pretty much."

She looks away and I realize I've unnecessarily made her feel an undeserved guilt. It's not the responsibility of a coffee-fetcher to save the world.

"Well, at least the government bureaucracy that you work for isn't charged with stopping this. That's a job for us heroes."

"Pretty much."

I smile at her. "Everyone serves, in some small way, even if they just fetch coffee. Help yourself. Liquid manna from heaven."

She looks around, probably uncomfortable at discussing the end of the world. "Looks almost like some kind of little heaven here. People working together, lifting each other up."

"No. Heaven's for heroes and angels. This is just people making the best of a bad situation."

"Maybe that's the same thing. Look at that woman over there, helping the young mothers take care of a crowd of kids. Yesterday when we came here, I saw her sitting on the side of the road with a WILL WORK FOR FOOD sign. Today, she has food and work. Her hands have a purpose. And everybody else is a little bit better off for it."

I look around.

Atlas and a couple of men are adding a lean-to onto the side of the Brainiac Center, using the tin roof, and lumber from a falling-down shed in the neighborhood. DB is cooking something that fills the air with the smells of . . . what? Cajun spices? Mediterranean vegetables? . . . in a big pot on a camp stove. Bleary-eyed Dulcinea is stirring the pot. There are hammering sounds from inside the Brainiac Center. A line of men and women are bringing food into the Q itself.

"It's just the Q. What we do here."

"And I'm just saying that it is still miraculous what you've done here."

"Me? No, this is not my mission. This just shows what people can do when they're threatened by something like a bomb."

"Every human being in a thousand miles is afraid of this bomb. But most are still going about their miserable, posturing lives, or showing their worst sides. Something else is happening here."

"Maybe."

Sancha and Chavez walk over.

Sancha is dancing back and forth with nervous energy. "Man, enough of this. I put out flyers yesterday while you were talking to your new friends, but nobody's called. We got to get out and ride around."

"We do. But first we've got to show kindness to these women, and help them with their coffee."

Zhong says, "Our coffee can wait. Maybe we can come with you."

"Yeah," Chavez says. "We heard you were an angel. I've always wanted to help an angel."

I light up like a Christmas tree.

"See, Sancha, I told you. Now everyone knows of our mission."

Sancha rolls her eyes.

"Now we have our first two disciples joining our mission, sent here by my father. The real one."

More eye-rolling.

"Don't they need to get coffee?"

I give Sancha the pitying look I've learned from her.

"Sancha, we have important work to do."

The women nod their heads.

"Whatever. Come with me."

Sancha drags us off and we all follow her into the storeroom. She closes the door behind us and talks to Chavez.

"Disciples or not, you got to promise not to tell anyone about this."

She reaches behind the canned goods and pulls out our black sweatshirts. Reaches back again and pulls out the stack of Depends.

I say, "Perhaps you should explain, Sancha."

"Better to show."

Chavez and Zhong look nervous until she pulls her shirt over her head and stuffs diapers into her shoulders.

"Thank God," says Chavez.

I grab my shirt and join in. Properly costumed, we present ourselves with a "ta-da" from Sancha.

Zhong reaches over and pulls up my hood. "So these are the mysterious superheroes."

"Angel," I frown.

Sancha says, "You in?"

Chavez nods.

Sancha says, "What you think, boss? We need a couple of costumes for these two?"

"I don't know. I'm kind of thinking that their tight black suit, skinny black tie look works for disciples."

As we walk through the Q, our steps fall together and I think of the cover on the Beatles old *Abbey Road* album. Dulcinea is taking a break, sitting on the shiny necklace box. She smiles at us.

"Stylin'."

Our bikes are plugged in around the side, charged and ready. Sancha pulls the tarp off.

"Our trusty steeds."

Chavez jerks her chin at their black sedan. "We'll follow in the supply wagon."

I straddle my steed and Sancha hands me the black two-by-four.

"He needs it for balance."

"My lance." I stab the night to demonstrate.

"Angelic," says Chavez.

"Mr. Noble American Angel, to you," says Sancha.

"Saddle up," I say.

Chavez and Zhong dash for their car, Chavez sliding over the hood, movie-style. I roll the power on and we ride off into the night.

day eight: 8:30 p.m.

the house-gobbling bomb

Where do you start looking for the end of the world? I realize that action without thought, even for a band of heroes, is just theater. But we've pulled out of the parking lot, with a cheering crowd behind us. I cannot hesitate and become a poor leader.

I make a forced, confident turn toward my house, figure it will be a good place to regroup and plan.

The streets are deserted, with just a few people drifting here and there. Few people, but a lot of trash. I swerve in and out of crushed boxes and garbage bags of belongings left behind. Sancha and I have no trouble avoiding the detritus of a city in terror, but what of the young women who have joined us in a car? I turn to check on them, lose my balance and have to swing my lance to stay upright.

Sancha ducks. "Watch it, boss." But all of us turn onto my street without incident. I see a neighbor sitting on her porch, rocking and humming. Nothing's going to harsh her mellow, even doomsday. I wave and she smiles, and then looks startled as she recognizes me. I pull to a stop in front of . . . nothing.

Nothing. I look at the number on the curb in front of the vacant lot. The number is my number. The houses on either side are my neighbors. But my house has ceased to exist, just like the house at 504 Greendale.

Maybe what happened to my past can happen to houses, too.

Sancha pulls up beside me. The two young women get out of their car and join.

"Sancha."

"Yeah, man. This is where you live. Lived. Whatever."

I look at the women. "Ms. Zhong, I swear, I lived in a house here, just yesterday."

They look at the ground, embarrassed. I can see they are questioning the sanity of the master they have chosen to follow. You think it's hard to convince people you're an angel without them thinking you're crazy, try convincing them that a house has disappeared. My neighbor comes over, huffing from the effort.

"Don, your house—wait, what happened to your shoulders?" She looks at Sancha's pads. "You too?"

She steps over to me and reaches for my neck. I flinch.

"I forgot," she says. "You don't like to be touched. Spoken to. Looked at. Easy boy."

She reaches in and pulls out a diaper. Shrugs.

"Carrying around spares? Not so crazy, with all the crap going on these days."

"You mean like bombs?"

"Bombs. Disappearing houses." She waves at the empty lot. "No idea what happened to your house. I went to check on my sister for a few hours. Came back and saw what you see. I looked away, looked back. Expected to see a house. Still do."

"You remember the house?"

"Of course I do. I can see you do, too. Nice little house. People always said to stay away from you. I said, 'For my money, any man takes care of his house has some good buried in him.' Still say it."

I look at the empty lot and force myself to see a house.

"Sometimes a thing is here yesterday, gone today, and lost maybe forever. Tell me, kind woman, what do you remember of me? Not the noble knight you see before you now, but the creature you knew in the days of old?"

"Days of old?" She laughs. "Well, noble knight, you were more like a troll. I'd smile and wave, and you'd growl—and I was probably your favorite. Parents told their kids to cross the street to avoid you. Always had a feeling you were like a ticking bomb, about to blow at any minute. And then you'd go away for weeks at a time." She smiles. "I never figured you were that bad. Well, sometimes I didn't."

But my mind has drifted, as all great minds do. I have divined an answer.

"I know what's going on," I say.

Sancha tries to step closer, but Zhong and her friend elbow her aside. They pull out small leather-covered notebooks and wait for me to speak.

"The bomb is taking houses one at a time. We must learn how this is done, so we can put an end to this and stop the bomb."

Sancha runs to the very green grass where my house had been. "No! No! This was done by men, Don, not magic." She reaches down, grabs two big handfuls of green blades, and yanks. The very earth comes up in a neat square. "Sod," she screams. "Would a bomb put down sod to cover its tracks? If we look, we can probably find a label from Home Depot."

The young women have put away their notebooks.

"Sancha, my very worthy squire. I think you must have a touch of the divine in you, as well. Of course, you are right."

She drops the sod and all of the women stare at me.

"Your hint is not wasted on me. To stop this monster, we must return to the roots."

My steed leaps into the night and they follow.

day eight: midnight

everything changes

My little town has changed. The last time Sancha and I made this trek together, Huntsville was in the middle of a warm May day. Now it is a very ugly night. Trash everywhere, cars wrecked and aban-doned in the street. Pillars of smoke rising around us. As we cross the Parkway, a band of young men run after us, shaking pieces of rebar and two-by-fours at us when we don't slow down.

I wonder how much of this was a change in the city, and how much a change in my vision. If the federal agents were right about my past, and maybe my evil, is this what the city looked like to me before? Is the divide in seeing that sharp? And which of me is right?

Another thought: is this the mean city my hateful ways had somehow made out of a spring-lovely community?

I want to stop to think, but the world is coming to an end.

We pull to a stop in front of what had been the house at 504 Greendale a few days ago. Sancha jumps off first and rips up another sod square.

"See? Remember what the people told us? Men came and did this."

I walk over and she points. Even in the night, I can see the remnants of a foundation that had been covered by the sod.

"This, too, made by men, Don. Men made it. Men destroyed it. No magic bombs needed for men to do evil."

"Perhaps," I nod. "It is hard for me to keep straight what I remember and what I imagine, what comes from heaven and what comes from earth."

Slowly, I turn around, trying to be sensitive to anything there is to see or remember. The visions pull into focus and then fade away, like trying to look at something close and something far away at the same time. I see the scene as it is today, vacant of physical structures but filled with questions. And then I see the house at night, from a time before: men in camouflage and rough clothes coming into the house under cover of night. I smell their sweat, and I almost see what happened inside of the house, hear the man who looked like me.

I try to hold on and learn more, but the vision clears and I am back to the empty lot. Four doors down I see Nigel, still here. He is in a garden, tending to a row of tomatoes by the light of the moon. Beside him on the ground, next to his garden tools, is a baseball bat. As he pulls weeds, he keeps one eye on us.

day 9: 1:00 a.m.

everything, all the time

As I walk toward him, he picks up the bat and watches us. As we get closer, he stares at the women in their black suits behind me, then drops the bat and stands with his hands out.

"Police?"

Chavez starts to say something but I speak first.

"No police. Friends."

She doesn't correct me. He looks skeptical, but says nothing.

"I'm surprised your family is still here. I thought you were leaving."

"My family's not here, mate. I sent them to my cousin's to the west."

"But you stayed?"

He studies me, not sure what he is seeing. Clearly, he has never seen a knight in full regalia.

"Come inside." He walks into the house and we follow him into a kitchen. He waits until the door is closed before he turns on the light.

"We still have electricity. Tea?"

Chavez says yes, please, and we all nod. When the tea is ready, we sit around the kitchen table.

"Yes," he finally says. "I stayed. I'm tired of running. Before the panic, I had work here helping people by building fine homes, and it meant something to them. My daughter has a school she loves. If this all blows up, my family will build a new life with my cousin. But if we survive here, they will come back, and we will fight together by more building. We decided. This is our country now, no matter what people say."

"But you will not run?"

"No."

"In the face of total destruction?"

"No."

"In the face of evil?"

"What kind? The men who took the house were not the same kind of evil as the men who used the house before, though they were both evil. The men who removed the house came in big trucks and helicopters and machines like I have never seen. And they were gone in a couple of hours. There is evil, in many forms, wherever you go."

Sancha says, "You told us about those men before. Who were the other men?"

He gestures at me. "The man who was maybe your father was there much of the time, often alone." He studies me. "Sometimes, sir, you came to his house for a while. But the other men were what scared me. White men in rough clothes.

Quiet going into the house, then loud voices and much cursing."

He studies me a little more. "There was a story about you—if you were his son—before my time. When the boy was younger, there was a neighbor, a retired librarian from a Catholic monastery. The librarian gave the boy books, and music, and the boy devoured them like water. Then the old man told the librarian not to give him words; he would plant bad seeds in the boy's mind. The librarian did not listen."

"What happened?"

He pointed toward the empty lot down the street. "Like the house, one day the librarian simply disappeared. But they said the boy would still sneak behind the house where his father could not see him, and escape into a world of library books and music and imagination. Perhaps he chose a world better than what he saw inside the house."

Chavez interrupts. "These men, were they there all the time?"

"No, more like a clubhouse. Meetings, maybe. Meetings that would start in the darkness and last all night."

I have a hunch. I pull out Sancha's flyer and put it on the table.

"Did these men ever bring anything that looked like this into the house?"

"No."

I feel Zhong and Chavez crowding close.

Chavez says something in Spanish that I do not understand.

"No," he says. "Why would rough blokes like these carry a hat box?"

I need to get this back on track.

"Have they been back since the house has been gone?"

"No, they all left before that. Sunday night, a week ago. They all came out of the house late, drunk and celebrating. Loaded up all the furniture from the house, piled in their trucks, and were gone."

I nod, "That was the night before my awakening."

I pat him on the shoulder.

"You are brave, my friend, and a heroic American knight in your own way. But just as you must fight by staying, we must fight by pursuing evildoers, and saving the world."

I realize I have slighted our women in black.

"And sometimes," I add for their benefit, "just by getting coffee."

Zhong turns red and Chavez balls up her fists. I turn back to the man.

"My noble friend, perhaps you can help us. You have seen both of these mysterious groups. We are in pursuit of whatever this evil is. What is it you see that we can fight?"

He looks at our little group with some sadness.

"Perhaps," he says, "it is too big. Perhaps there is nothing to fight."

"No! We fight it all. Everything, all the time."

Sancha rolls her eyes. "Now your divine inspiration is coming from Glen Frey and the Eagles. Some music that priests gave you."

An explosion rocks the earth and the windows flash behind the curtains. I go to the window and peek out at a huge plume of black smoke hanging in the air.

"See? The evil calls us."

We run out, and back to our mounts. I push my steed into action, feeling almost as if my little scooter is pawing the air and neighing.

day 9: 5:00 a.m.

saving detective harriette

My steed, like me, is growing weary, but she gives me all she can. Our little band of heroes push across the Parkway at Bob Wallace Avenue, all the traffic from this once-busy crossroads drained away like blood from a corpse. The black cloud is rising against the moon. If this is the bomb, and if it's as powerful as the TV has told me, we have to get there before it grows. The road ends at a fence around the Lowe Mill Arts Center. I stop.

The cloud has dissipated at the ground, leaving a charred circle as it floats upward, like a dark angel threatening heaven itself.

"I thought it would be bigger."

Sancha says, "No, man, that's not *the* bomb. Just a bomb. Or an accident. Or . . . man, if that was the bomb they're talking about, our whole world would have disappeared."

"Ah, I've had that happen."

"No. No you have not. You got some bad drugs, or ate a week-old hot dog at the Q, man, and freaked out and haven't recovered. Look at the people down there. That's what the whole city looks like now. And that's just fear doing that, man, not the bomb. This is like John the Baptist saying the big thing is on its way."

Lowe Mill was an old textile mill converted to an arts center, and was usually boiling with the energy of young dreamers and hippies and crazy people doing every kind of art you could and could not imagine. Now, the old building is dark except for one street light in the parking lot. Around the charred spot, the Lowe Mill artists have turned from the war of art to the art of war. One tiny young woman in a sarong swings a bronze statue at a much larger boy with a scruffy beard, and a head flies off. Fortunately, it's the statue's head, but the big guy is still unconscious before he hits the ground. On the edge of the crowd, a man with purple hair pulls a gun and shoots into the crowd, just as someone stabs him with what looks like an ancient spear. This is a war with no sides and no apparent purpose except to kill, and maybe survive.

"Fear sure seems to be working."

Sancha points. "Look."

In the middle stands a small older woman dressed in black, fighting to separate the warring parties. She pushes two young men apart, and one kicks her in the back for her trouble. She straightens up, and picks another pair to separate, at least temporarily.

Harriette.

"A damsel in distress." I kick through a gap in the fence and scream, "In the name of all that's holy." Sancha joins with a much louder unintelligible scream, followed by Chavez and then Zhong.

The people on the edge of the crowd look up at the screaming banshees flying down the hill toward them. They freeze, arms raised in mid-slash holding various object d'art and stare open-mouthed at us. Then one drops her vase and runs, followed by another and another until the war has disappeared like the puff of smoke that called us here.

Leaving only Harriette.

"What's up, Officer?" says Sancha.

"Just what I thought would happen. Artists are all peaceful and cooperative, but underneath they are boiling with fire and competitiveness. I thought this might be the time this would boil over."

"So you came by yourself?"

Shrugs. "Only cop left in town. Somebody's got to do it."

"I think you're more than a cop, Harriette. I think you're a hero, too."

She laughs. "Let's hope the real heroes out there are shutting this bomb down."

We need that hero. And all I'm doing is scaring children.

day nine: 6:00 a.m.

tilting at windmills for fun and profit

Why is it so hard to save the world? I've been sent here with a mission that is clear, but given no superpowers to accomplish my mission. Instead of saving the world—a worthy mission for a heroic angel—I'm breaking up small fights and trying to hold together my tiny band of stout-hearted but limited warriors.

And then I feel ashamed. It's a poor workman who blames his tools. I look back at our entourage: Sancha beside me, followed by Chavez riding with Harriette, since Zhong has been called to another pointless meeting of her government job. Great American Heroes, every one of them. In a world literally going to hell in a hand basket, they have chosen to stand and fight rather than do the sensible thing and run. I hold up my hand and pull to a stop in front of a deserted putt-putt golf course. I look at the three of them and my heart swells with pride at what the people in this place can be.

None of them can fly. None can see through walls, or even find something as large as an atomic bomb. I don't think anyone but Harriette even has a gun.

But here they are. At this moment I think there is only one superpower—the ability to see that something is wrong, and find the courage to stand up to it.

And if I don't save my heroes, they're all going to die. Soon, and with a lot of other people.

Despite my whining, I realize the superpowers I have been given are faith and a heart. My heart called me into this world, somehow. When I listened to it, it captured a drug dealer and freed women from bondage. And my faith tells me now that I have all the powers I need to save the world, if I will just be still and listen.

I shut out my doubts, and close my eyes and breathe slowly. An image slowly forms in my mind: the bomb from Sancha's poster, standing upright on its fins like a man-sized rocket about to launch. Gaining confidence in my powers, I open my eyes. The bomb remains, superimposed on the land-scape that is emerging in the dawn like a video game with multiple layers. I hold my arms up, summoning every feeble power within and without me. I chant "Om," figuring I need every advantage I can get. Slowly, keeping my neck and shoulders locked to avoid disrupting my second sight, I rotate with my feet only, praying my faith will give me miraculous guidance.

Nothing. I do a full rotation with nothing to show for it. Maybe this is a mistake.

I am losing my faith when I hear a chorus of "Oms" and I focus closer on Sancha. Despite her doubts, she has her arms up, joining me in the sound of the universe, tears streaming down her face, praying with a desperation and a faith in my mission that has her eyes on fire. I rotate a little more to Chavez, the skepticism showing in her face but still straining to reach for heaven and joining our one-note song with all the enthusiasm she can muster. Finally, I come to Harriette, hands up with her sad eyes filled with a prayer more powerful than the years of defeat she has known.

Strengthened, I raise my tiny yawp to heaven, shift my gaze a little lower, and continue circling for another round.

There! My faith is rewarded! There is a small flash in my vision, just a tiny blip. But I listen to it, slow down, backtrack and the blip becomes a steady glow surrounding an object exactly the size and orientation of the bomb. The bomb must be hiding in there. I drop my arms. It is time for faith to give birth to works.

"Monster!" I challenge. "Creature of evil! Prepare to meet your doom."

I pick up my lance, kick my steed into action, and charge the windmill on the putt-putt course, which is undoubtedly hiding the bomb. My scooter reaches its top speed and I feel I am flying with all of the powers of truth, justice, and the

American way focused into the tip of my lance, which is glowing like a fiery sun. I scream at the top of my lungs at the moment of impact, and black out.

I smile as I regain consciousness, much as I did eight days ago in the Q. This time, I know I will awaken in heaven, looking down on my band of happy warriors dancing in a pile of shattered pieces of the bomb and the windmill.

Instead, Sancha is staring into my eyes.

"Man, you alive? You're one crazy dude sometimes."

I look around. My lance lies broken and useless on the ground. The windmill has fallen over, its blades still turning. I can see inside. There is no bomb.

We can all see everything.

Sancha says, "C'mon, boss. Let's go home."

Chavez picks me up. Harriette puts my broken scooter into her trunk.

As they load me into the back of the car, I look Sancha in the eye.

"Faith and works, Sancha."

"Yeah, boss."

time to boom 6:00:00

oh, by the way

Zhong slouches into the back of the FBI conference room, sipping a cup of coffee picked up from the Q and studying the boards. Bannon, standing at the podium, spies her and glares.

"Did you bring enough for everyone?"

"No."

He gives another glare, but when she ignores it he replaces it with a John Wayne thousand-yard stare, which says that he is an important man about to give an important speech.

"Heroes of the Bureau, we expect to face big challenges because we're Americans, and our challenge has just gotten bigger. Our crack analysis team has completed their examination of the data that was uploaded in the few seconds that the bomb was out in the open yesterday." He holds up a thick document. "It will take them a day to release the full report and put it on the secure website for you to download, but there is one important fact that I can tell you now."

He pauses for dramatic effect. The effect he gets is that several agents stop playing solitaire (the secure Federal version of the app) on their phones and look up.

"When the bomb was out of its case, it was set for a timed detonation of thirty hours. The bomb has been activated and is now counting down."

Several men sit up straight. Several others do not.

"Based on this, we have gone on full alert. Mr. Pilgrim is boarding the Airborne Command Center as we speak, to ensure that we have an unbroken chain of command. And, because we still have not located the manual, which has the code that the bomb must be set to in order to disarm the bomb, we have brought in the XJ-275 Mobile Destruction Center."

The big screen shows a picture of an olive-green armored vehicle with a thick metal box on the back, and a conical top like a funnel narrowing to a pipe. "When the bomb is located, do not waste any time trying to disarm it. It must immediately be placed into the opening in the back of this vehicle and the 'initiate' button must be pressed. This will seal the chamber and safely dispose of the device by vaporization."

Bannon raises his voice.

"Your assignments will be distributed as soon as we complete the clearance process. Under emer-gency rules, anyone refusing an assignment or attempting to leave will be shot."

He pulls his pistol out and sets it on the podium.

Zhong stands up. "There's only one very slim chance of stopping this thing, and it ain't in this room. Shoot me if you want, but I'm going back to work."

Bannon puts his hand on his gun.

A voice in the back says, "Let her go. We don't need coffee anyway."

Bannon shrugs. "She's not important. Oh, by the way, because the report on the bomb is an official government document, it had to go through the White House clearance process to ensure that nothing in the report supported global warming or endangering the lives of unborn children. Because our president personally intervened, that clearance was completed in an unbelievably fast twenty-four hours. This leaves us . . ." Several members of the team count on their fingers, and look up shocked when they get to the first finger of the second hand. ". . . six hours. Or so."

A couple of agents jump up and draw their weapons. A couple sit down and put their heads in their hands. Zhong jogs for the door. She looks back at the big board one last time. It reads TIME TO BOOM: 6:00:00. As she watches, it clicks to 5:59:59. She slips out the door as men start screaming.

time to boom 5:31:00

ain't but one way out, baby

"I do need to sleep," I tell Dulcinea. "But I don't need to be asleep. A world I was sent to save only eight days ago could blow up at any moment."

Sancha joins in. "Boss, maybe she's right. That monster of a windmill beat you up pretty bad." She looks away. "And I don't think attacking golf hazards with a two-by-four is going to save the day here."

"No."

But I still stand in front of the coffee pot, my hand on a cup as it fills. I pray that enough liquid fire will wake something useful in me.

Chavez is on Sancha's computer. "Get some sleep, man. More slapstick isn't going to save the day. Maybe sleep will work; wake up something in your brain. Maybe Zhong and the Lost Boys will come up with something—miracles happen. Maybe the bomb's not even here anymore."

Dulcinea takes the cup and replaces it with her hand.

"Come, my angel. Let's find you a cloud somewhere."

Maybe they're right. I do know that I've committed myself to being ruled by this wondrous hand she's offering. And I am oh, so tired.

"All right."

Zhong bursts in the door. "Chavez! We've only got . . ." She looks at her watch. "Five hours and thirty-two minutes. No. Five-thirty-one."

Chavez stands up. "What do you mean?"

"The bomb is ticking. It's going off in—"

"Yeah. I get it. What's going on at the bomb center?"

"Lot of boys changing their shorts. Hopefully not shooting each other in the ass. We're the only hope. The. World. Is. Ending. Now."

With effort, I drop Dulcinea's hand.

"You? You're just coffee runners." I realize how rude that sounds. Kindness counts, even at the end of the world. "Very nice, well dressed coffee runners. And my favorite disciples. But—"

"And you're . . . I don't know what you are. But whatever you are, you are our only chance. Chavez and I work for the government organization in charge of finding the device—"

"And you've been focused on coffee?"

"Yeah. And you need to focus, right now."

She walks over, finishes filling the cup, and puts it in my hand.

"Chug that, straight. We need to get as much of that as possible in you to maybe jar something lose. If you don't have the answer in your brain, nobody does."

I pour the whole cup straight down and then scream as my throat turns to dragon fire. I shove the cup at her.

"More."

She fills up the cup. Dulcinea says, "Wait," and mercifully drops in some ice from the drink fountain. I chug that one, too, and feel like my stomach is full of snakes.

"More."

A couple more cups and then I'm spilling more coffee around my mouth than I get down my throat. I hold out the cup but Dulcinea pushes it away.

"Enough."

She drags a stool over and puts me on it. My stomach is so large I feel like a golf ball on a tee.

Zhong studies my face.

"Anything?"

"Yeah. I feel like I'm going to throw up."

Chavez says, "Maybe we can read his vomit like tea leaves. It's as good a chance as we've got."

Zhong says, "No. Hold it in. Let it work. Some-thing jolted your brain one way, we need something to jolt it back."

She puts her face in mine.

"Think."

Dr. Brainiac walks up. He fills his cup, takes a sip, and watches us both.

"Zhong," I say. "I told the FBI everything I know, and it didn't help them. I've been honest with all of you about everything."

"I know that. You are nothing if not honest, Don. But there's something more inside that skull of yours. Sometimes, you are very intelligent and sophisticated, and seem to have connections to every wise thing on earth. And then you are utterly clueless."

"Thank you?"

Dr. Brainiac is listening intently to both of us, his head swiveling back and forth like someone with a large bet on a tennis match.

Zhong says, "No, I mean it. There's something in there, something you know but can't get to. There's got to be."

"You think I don't know this? How about the fact that my house and my father's house were both taken by the bomb, and no one knows why?"

"Well—"

"But Sancha went through my father's house. There was no bomb there. Not even a garage or any good place big enough to hide a bomb. That leaves my little house. My memory is good enough to tell you everything that was in there, and there was no bomb. Zhong, I am not holding out on you—on any of you."

"Yeah, I know. I'm not blaming you. But there are so many connections to you, there's got to be something—"

"We're going round and round, going nowhere. Like everything else I've done. You want more from me? Tell me what to do. What do any of you want from me? I'm dropped here with nothing and you treat me like I have everything and—"

Dr. Brainiac says in a very quiet way that somehow makes us all listen.

"Perhaps I can help."

time to boom 3:00:00

junkie skills

It takes a couple of hours for Sancha and Chavez to scramble around and get what the doctor needs. Zhong is muttering, "Three hours. Three damned hours to live and I'm spending it in a convenience store."

Dr. Brainiac waves her silent and speaks to me. "This is the anti-amnesiac I told you about. There's no guarantee. Of anything. I'll repeat my warning: You could remember everything. Or nothing. You could be old Don. Or new Don. Or . . . nothing. There is real danger here."

I say, "Like getting blown up?"

He sighs. "Since we don't know what happened to you, we don't know what this will do. I just want you to know everything before you make your decision."

Dulcinea is holding my hand, and she's shaking. "I don't think you should do this, Don. I don't want to lose you."

I squeeze. "And I don't want all of us to lose everything."

I am lying on a torn army cot in the corner of the Brainiac Center. The doctor has draped a couple of tie-dyed sheets from the ceiling to give us a kind of dirty, psychedelic hospital cubicle. He's playing with an IV bag, walking his hands along the plastic line that comes out of it and leads to a needle, mercifully still in its sterile packaging. He looks like a kid on Christmas morning with a new toy that he's trying to put together without the instructions.

Dulcinea says, "You've done this before?"

"Sure." He reads the printing on the needle packaging. "Ah." He turns it around the other way. "At least, my nurse used to do this. Or the anesthesiologist's nurse did. Someone in the operating room did it."

He sets the needle down on the pizza box we're using as a surgical tray. Dulcinea has wiped it down lightly with hot water, so we're calling it sterile.

"Here's the deal. There are a class of drugs called amnesiacs. They're used to knock patients out for minor procedures. If you've ever had a colonoscopy, you've had them."

I start to get up. "You're not doing a colonoscopy on me. Some things are worse than the end of the world."

He pushes me back.

"No, I wouldn't know which end to . . . Never mind. Anyway, to bring you back after the procedure, sometimes they give you an anti-amnesiac." He gestures at the bag. "Like this." He squints at the bag for a moment. "Yeah, like this."

Dulcinea puts her hand on the inside of my elbow, blocking the vein.

"And maybe we lose this good Don that we've got. We don't know if this will work. Even if it works, and Don remembers who he is, we don't know that man. And we all need this one."

Zhong puts her hand on Dulcinea's. "Even if old Don may be the only hope of saving the world?"

"For me, yes. I'll take new Don over the world."

But she moves her hand. Dr. Brainiac swabs my arm with disinfectant. He takes the needle and makes two pointless holes in my arm without finding a vein.

"Looked easy when nurses did it."

Dulcinea takes the needle. "Give me that."

She slides the needle in painlessly, and the world blinks out.

time to boom 2:00:00

perched above, looking down

I open my eyes to a room full of the stupidest people I've ever seen. They are gathered in an idiotic circle staring down at me. A tall Chinese woman is shaking me.

"Wake up, Don. We don't have time for you to sleep."

I shake her arm away. "What the hell are you jackasses looking at?"

I sit up and rip the IV out of my arm. Blood spurts all over my clothes and I glare at them.

"Now look what you've done."

I'm in some kind of a tutti-fruiti-colored hell with people I vaguely recognize. I jump off the bed, snatch one of the hippie curtains down, and wad it onto my arm to stop the bleeding.

"Hey," says a man wearing a woman's kimono with tropical flowers on it. Somehow, I know his name. Dr. Brainiac. Clearly false advertising.

"Hey, yourself." Wait. With the Technicolor curtain down, I see the old Laundromat. See it behind new tables and chairs and . . . people.

"Get out!" I pick up a folding chair and throw it at a mother and a baby. "This is my father's Laun-dromat. If we wanted people, we'd put up a big goddamn welcome sign. Jesus."

The tall Chinese woman—Zhong is her name—gets between me and the mother and child.

I kick her. "Get them out of here, you god-damned foreigner! Get them all out. No people, anywhere. Get them all out. Now."

Her partner, Chavez, another foreigner, steps in front of me.

"Sir, we need information from you. Fast."

I ignore her until she puts a hand on my arm, clearly thinking that will establish some kind of kumbaya bond. Clearly, she's wrong.

A scream comes out of me like some kind of beast from a hell of tortured souls. She jumps back.

"Don't touch me."

I pull away.

Chavez says, "Sir, you've got to stop."

The one called Sancha says to her, "Wait."

I've got to get somewhere safe. I run out. At the door, I become tangled in a banner. Pulling myself out, I see the banner is an old sheet painted in the same new-age colors as the sheets inside.

The banner says WELCOME.

I scream again, pull the banner down and stomp on it, yelling, "No! No! No!"

Run next door to my familiar Quick Stop.

Full. Of. People. And lights.

"Who put all these lights up?"

I throw cans at the lights, bulbs pop and shards of glass rain down, and people run out in blessed fear. I make it around the counter to my familiar hiding place. I pop all of the bulbs back here and put my hand on my safe lifeguard's chair. An ugly woman puts three ears of corn on the counter and drops money into a plastic bucket in front of me. I turn the bucket around and read the words.

"No! My father does not give things away in his store, like some kind of communist. You want something, you pay for it, in the cash register, like an honest citizen." I push the corn onto the floor. "And we don't sell crap like that. You want corn, you take a can off the shelf like an American."

Sancha is standing in the door holding back the two women in black, along with the doctor and a scrawny hag.

"Give him a second. This is old Don. Screams at everyone, climbs into his comfy spot, and goes to sleep."

I climb up into the lifeguard's chair, curl up, and the world blessedly disappears. Again.

time to boom 1:00:00

i tried

They think I'm sleeping, but I'm not. Here, inside my head, is the only place I can be alone and get away from all the idiots.

I hear them out there, muttering, plotting stupidly against me the way the whole world always has. I don't know what to do. Hiding seems like a good option.

Then a shock of water hits me and I splutter awake.

"Sorry," says Zhong, bucket in hand. I shake my head but it's all . . . different now. The world swirls, dissolves, reforms. I feel like I'm waking up again.

Then I see the most beautiful thing I have ever seen.

"Dulcinea."

I hop down.

"Dulcinea, my queen, you're crying." I take her hands in mine. "How can this humble servant slay the dragons that have put sadness in the source of all the world's beauty?"

Chavez says, "This is nuts."

Dr. Brainiac says, "You're right. Somehow, we've got the old Don and the new Don, but they're not communicating."

"Still nuts."

"Called multiple personalities."

Dulcinea says, "You were mean. No. You were gone and . . . someone else was here."

"Sounds like you, my queen. You are royalty, until the drugs take over. Maybe this is why I can see the queen in you when others can't."

"Maybe. Please don't go away again. We need the good Don here."

"I won't." I look at the doctor. "Is this something I can control?"

He shrugs.

"Dulcinea, you know about living in two worlds: There is Dulce, who needs . . . things, and Dulcinea, my noble queen. How do you control going back and forth?"

She looks down.

"I don't know. I didn't know there was a Dulcinea in me until you called her out."

Someone grabs me by the shoulders, and I'm facing Chavez.

"I don't care who you are or who you're preten-ding to be, but control it now. We've got one hour. One hour until the world ends. We need answers, and we need to talk to the one who's got them."

She slaps me and something pops in my head again.

"Stupid government bureaucrat bitch," I say. "Get out of my way."

"Gladly, you fruitcake, when you tell us where the bomb is."

She slaps me, hard again. Something pops again.

"Zounds! How could a true disciple do such a thing to her master? You must have had a very good reason. And I will know the reason for this, now."

"Where is the bomb? We have sixty minutes to live, and you—one of you—is the only one who knows where it is. Enough of these stupid games."

They are all gathered around me now and I can feel their anger and disappointment and panic. I'm hurt, but I understand. They've turned to me for leadership and I've given them nothing. Against certain doom, I offered them a broken piece of lumber and a crazy sideshow. Instead of angels and heroes, I gave them clerks hiding in diapers.

"I don't know. I can't give any more."

I feel the world pressing on me like a vice. "But I tried."

I know where I go when I feel like this. I climb up into my lifeguard's chair, close my eyes, and fade away. Fade away, and, for the first time, pray for my own oblivion.

time to boom 0:45:00

hiding place

There may be peace on the other side of the grave, but there is none here.

"Stop shaking me, bitch." I withdraw further away from the local junkie who seems to think I'm her personal rag doll. "Go take another hit of that battery acid that will rot the skin off your bones and let you die a blessed death. Then get the hell out of my way."

She turns and commands them all.

"Get out of here. This is between Don and me."

Chavez says, "This isn't working. Both halves of him are bat-shit crazy."

But she walks away. The rest follow.

Dulcinea puts a hand on my chest and says, "Wait."

I start to push her hand away but somehow I cannot.

"I need to speak to the angel in you."

I can, however, sneer.

"You haven't been paying attention, Queenie. No angels here in my personal hell."

"I've paid attention to your every word for the last eight days. You awakened me, as surely as you were awakened. Every day, after I passed out, you would whisper a blessing in my ear, even though you thought I was sleeping. But I heard, every word. Though my body tried to sleep, the angel in me heard every word."

I sneer.

She puts her hand on my lips.

"I listened to you. Now you need to listen to yourself. This is what you said to me, every day, with no reason to believe my ears would hear, but with hope that it would go straight to my heart, because you said it with love. It did. Now it's your turn. Listen:

"May God bless you with discomfort
At easy answers, half-truths,
and superficial relationships
So that you may live deep within your heart.

"May God bless you with anger
At injustice, oppression,
and exploitation of people
So that you may work for justice,
freedom, and peace.

"May God bless you with tears
To shed for those who suffer pain,
rejection, hunger, and war
So that you may reach out to comfort them and
To turn their pain into joy.

"And may God bless you with enough foolishness
To believe you can make a difference in the world
So you can do what others claim cannot be done
To bring justice and kindness to all our people
and the poor."

She took her hand down, but I didn't move.

I remembered the prayer. "The Franciscan Benediction." Like most good prayers, it is less a call to God than to the best part of ourselves, living deep in our own hearts. Many years ago, a man like an angel taught it to me. My father beat me when I recited it to him. But I still said it to myself, every night."

She nods. "And yet, that same father gave the man in you all the pain you needed to make the first part of this come true."

I don't say anything.

She is holding both of my hands. "Like all of us, you've been trying to decide if you're an angel or a man. But now we need the angel and the man to unite."

I could feel my stupid eyes becoming wet.

"No angels here, sister."

"I've seen him."

"You haven't seen the things I've done."

"That's what being a man is about. Standing up to that is what makes a man an angel."

She pauses and I wait.

She says, "Sometimes angels are just ordinary people who help us believe in miracles again."

I smile, "That came from Anna Grace Taylor."

"You've read a lot. Connected with a lot of angel-people, even if everything outside of books in your world told you men were devils. Every wise thing has probably been said by an angel-person before. But you've got to be a man to bring them together in your heart."

I try hard. Fuzzy shapes float through my mind like ghosts, some of them crystalizing into memo-ries. Some not.

"I don't know. There was something big going on that my father wouldn't tell me about. But he said I would be the one to bring the world its final glory. I know his men put something in my base-ment, but when I went down, there was no bomb there."

"If your brain won't give you the answer, then don't think. Relax. Let your feelings talk to you." She reaches out and closes my eyes. "Now."

When I open them, I say, "I know where the bomb is."

When I see the hope in her smile, I add, "Maybe."

time to boom 0:30:00

something goes up in smoke

"You're kidding," says Zhong.

We're standing in front of an orange storage locker a hundred yards from the Q.

Chavez says, "Don't slow him down. We've only got thirty minutes left."

There is a rumbling thunder behind us. The biggest military vehicle I've ever seen pulls up with a small conical hat on top that makes me think of the tin man from *The Wizard of Oz*. A soldier jumps out. Chavez yells, "Get that door open, soldier, just in case."

She turns to me and gestures at the padlock on the door.

"Open it. Now."

"I don't have the key. And I'm really not sure of this. You say the bomb was in my house, but I never saw it there, and now my house is gone. This is where my father's group stored mock-ups of things that they used for training, and any junk they didn't have a home for. Maybe they hid the bomb here. Maybe not. But it's the only place I can think of. Really, maybe we should just—"

She pulls her gun out and shoots the lock off. "Less talking."

As soon as the door is open, I can see that I've failed on a monstrous scale. There are cardboard silhouettes of recent presidents, with bullet holes in them. A row of helmets, flak jackets, a model of the neighborhood around the White House, with string for sight lines, and a plywood mock-up of a bank vault that we were going to rob, until I screwed up the plan.

But nothing like the bomb from Sancha's flyer. Nothing that big. Zhong studies the pile of discarded training mockups.

"There!" she yells.

She snatches up a hat box like the one Dulcinea's necklace is in, but a little cheaper-looking. Runs to the monster vehicle with Chavez close behind and hurls it into the open door. Chavez slaps an olive-drab button the size of a pizza. The door slides shut and the whole vehicle starts to whir and shake. As the whirring becomes a high-pitched screech, we cover our ears. When we can't stand it anymore, the whirring stops. There is an almost-silent pop, and a tiny puff of red, white, and blue smoke belches out of the little hat and floats skyward.

Chavez and Zhong are high-fiving.

"Why? What?" I say.

"We've saved the world," Chavez says.

"No, you—"

I stop. I'm not sure of anything right now.

"Trust us." Zhong is grinning with more emotion than I've ever seen from her. "We 'government bureaucrats' know things."

time to boom 0:00:00

the end

"Trust us," Chavez echoes.

"I do, Chavez. Really. It's just . . ."

We are walking back into the Q to celebrate our salvation.

"We saved your ass." She looks at her watch. "If not for us, you would be imaginary angel dust in seven minutes. You men just can't handle being saved by women."

"Maybe. I'm not sure of anything now. The flood of human and angel memories fighting for control of us brings a disconcerting confusion to those of us living on this Earth. I liked being a pure angel better. It's hard to be human."

"Get used to it."

"Maybe."

Seven minutes until the end of the world. I look around for what I would want for that brief flicker of life, if the bomb was still out there.

"Dulcinea."

I take her hand. It is a bold move, but I'm not sure that the meek are going to have an earth to inherit. I drop to one knee, but Sancha bumps me and offers a plastic, two-liter wine bottle.

I stand up. "C'mon, Dulcinea. We need some privacy."

I take her by the hand and lead her into the storeroom. I arrange a couple of the cleanest boxes and set her down on them. I see the hat box with her necklace and set it on the floor next to her. I get down on one knee.

"Beautiful lady, light of my life. 'A time comes when you need to stop waiting for the man you want to become to show up, and start acting like the man you want to be.'"

I smile and add, "I know that came from Bruce Springsteen, a man, but a man who listened to the angel in him. And now, I want to be both an angel and a man. The angel in me has confessed his devotion to the queen in you. But it's time for the man in me to confess his love to you, and to ask you to share whatever little time we have together on this often miserable Earth, devoted as angels and royals fulfilling our heavenly missions together, hand in hand until the universe blows us into dust, noble in our love even in that final flicker."

She smiles a smile and the thousand suns in her eyes sparkle, and I think perhaps the world has exploded but no, it is her grace. And something more.

She puts her hand on my cheek and my body is filled with the warmth of those suns.

"Noble angel who has come from heaven to save me from hell. I, too, love you—the angel and the man. But—"

She looks around the room and spots the jewelry box. Opens it. The necklace is pulsing faster and faster, the colors glowing with an unearthly power now. She takes the necklace out and holds it. The necklace is flashing almost continuously, and a high-pitched note rises as she puts it around her neck.

"I love you, but I am not worthy of you. I am not an angel, or even a queen. But you've showed me how a man can be an angel, so perhaps I can learn to be a queen. I have much to work on. Someday, my love, I will work them all out and we will be angels and queens together, and I will wear this token of our heavenly love forever."

"You are already my angel and my queen. Even if it is just for this moment, this moment will last forever."

She reaches up and takes the necklace off.

"It will, my lord. But until I'm worthy, we'll keep the symbol of our love back in its safe place. And I will treasure this moment as dearly as if it were my last."

She holds the necklace in her lap for a moment. The sound turns into a screech so powerful that I cover my ears. She puts it in the case and takes my hand. We both stare together at the beautiful glowing symbol of our loving mission, and smile with our own glow that will last forever while the necklace begins to light the room like a rising sun.

She sees something in the necklace and takes her hand away from me. She picks up the necklace and studies the words. Smiles at me through the deafening roar of this new world.

"These are not the words for angels to live by. We need words to stand for us, until the end of time."

She rotates the letters, changing a single letter one at a time. The noise and the light grow as she works. The concrete walls are shaking and small pieces rain down around us.

I don't care. I am an angel, and I have my queen.

Bigger chunks of concrete are falling on us as I see the last letter click into place.

Love^All.

The necklace goes silent and fades to a warm glow, and the world stops shaking.

She puts the necklace back in the box, and we hide the talisman of our quest of love in a hidden corner of the room.

epilogue

the hero's journey

"You're glowing," says Sancha as Dulcinea and I walk out of the storeroom, hand in hand.

"It is from my heart."

"No, Don, really, both of you are . . . Never mind. This man is here to see you."

There is a tall man in a severely tailored black suit with a black homburg hat. He holds a black umbrella in one hand and a slim black briefcase in the other.

"Mister Donald Tiberius Becker, Junior?"

"I was called that, before my mission."

He hangs his umbrella on the chewing tobacco rack and takes the handkerchief from his breast pocket. Wipes down the bits of fallen concrete from the counter and sets the briefcase on it. With a deft little move, he pops the latches, opens the case, and takes out a sheaf of papers.

"Mister Donald Tiberius Becker, Senior has chosen to be dead. He has chosen to leave you, his only son, the deed and responsibility for the property known as the Quick Stop Emporium and Laundromat." He puts the papers down on the briefcase and extracts a solid gold pen from inside his jacket. "Sign here."

"'Chosen to be dead'?"

"That is what I was informed. Sign here and I'll be on my way."

I do, and he is. Then thumb through the stack of incomprehensible legal papers and come to a brown paper towel, with sloppy handwriting on it. I unfold it and read:

> Little Jackass,
>
> If you're reading this, you didn't do your job. I put the handwritten envelope with clear instructions on where to find the bomb, and what to do to set it for a thirty-hour deton-ation, in your mailbox. The first line was, 'Be a good boy, and set that last letter for your dear old Dad.' If you're reading this, you didn't. You've never done a single task right, but I hoped you would get this first big assignment right. But you're no hero, Don.

I look away and think about the empty envelope in the trash. Now, I remember the contents. And I remember being torn between false pride and real shame.

> I hoped you would grow up and take my organization of QAnon and turn it into a beautiful and powerful Q to change America. But you screwed up and now you're left with the most screwed-up place in the screwed-up world for your kingdom.
>
> The joke is on you. Your now-heavenly father has sentenced you to hell in the Quick Stop. The same loser of a convenience store I set so my twenty-two-year-

> old loser of a son could have a job and stay out of my house. Now, it's all yours. You deserve each other.

I laugh. It's funny, but I don't know why, like a joke with a big lead-up and a punchline that you don't get but the whole world is laughing about. Maybe the slapstick is the innocent child in each of us, slipping and sliding along the banana peels our parents have strewn for us, trying to overcome it all by doing something great without realizing that the secret is not greatness, but simple, everyday goodness. After all this drama, is this all my grand mission is to be? Day-to-day service, while the world is always one hour from a destruction that I can never comprehend, but am always honor-bound to fight?

Maybe.

And maybe I did build a beautiful Q to change America.

yet another epilogue

god bless

Bob Pilgrim stands at the podium of the Huntsville Hilton in front of a room full of TV cameras. He is flanked on one side by Chavez and Zhong. On the other, a small boy, his grandson, sits in a highchair playing with a rattle. A cynical man would suggest that the child was there to humanize the politician, but that would be, well, cynical. "Ladies and gentlemen," he says.

"We are here to present you the story of how the true American heroes of the FBI have yet again saved all of the American people." He pauses. "With the direction of the Great American President. In a few minutes, we will premiere a short film dramatizing the efforts of Agents Chavez and Zhong here. In recognition of the importance of their actions, Hollywood has cast two of its finest actresses, Charlize Theron and Reese Witherspoon, to play their parts.

"And. in recognition of their skill and dedication, Agents Chavez and Zhong have been appointed as extra-special agents, authorized to take any actions needed to protect American values, including breaking any and all laws, and accountable only to the president.

"Now, if you'll all retire to the ballroom, before the film we have refreshments provided by Alabama's own George Wallace Café, which serves any American—

except for gays, lesbians, Muslims, hippies, Democrats, Mexican, Chinese . . ." He squints at the teleprompter. "And anyone who listens to the music of Bruce Springsteen or Steely Dan. Thank you."

As the press drifts next door, Pilgrim pulls Chavez and Zhong to the baby.

"My grandson," he says proudly.

"Very handsome," said Zhong.

"See that rattle? That's a one of a kind. That was the remote control for the device, before you destroyed it. You set the device by rotating the beads on the rattle. Get one pattern right, and it would flash to let you know that you were on track. Get ten right, and boom. Harmless now, of course. Wanted him to get used to having the scepter of power in his hands. We're grooming him to be president someday."

The baby coos and twists the rattle. The rattle flashes red and he coos louder.

Pilgrim is proud. "Bright boy. Takes after his grandfather. He'll make America safe someday."

acknowledgements

It's rare for a book to be brought into existence by a not-so-silent partner, but *Don of the Q* was. Grace Treutel inspired, nagged, shaped, edited, and loved each and every chapter to life, even when I was too tired to believe I would ever finish this book. Thanks, Grace. Don and I both look forward to the day when we will stand in a very long line to buy your book.

Stacy Pethel and Amanda Campbell have been instrumental in every book I've ever done, giving me multiple passes of detailed comments and insights, helping pick covers and readers and—this time—even offering to sacrifice one of their children. Leigh Daniel shared insights and beer and made Don better.

Lisa Wysocky, the world's greatest editor and equestrian, corrected mistake after mistake of mine tirelessly.

Ruslan Us took a few contradictory ideas and created a great cover. James Woodrich did a great job of bringing to life all of the characters for the audiobook.

And Pat Leary Guillebeau always brings more love, to everything from beginning to end, than anyone else I've ever known.

Thank you all.

about the author

Michael Guillebeau is the author of six novels and two short story anthologies. His book, *MAD Librarian*, won the 2017 Foreword Reviews Indie Award for Humor. Guillebeau has published over thirty-five short stories, including three in *Ellery Queen's Mystery Magazine.* He lives in Madison, Alabama and Panama City Beach, Florida.

Free stuff for you!

I've included the first chapter from two of my books for you to sample.

And more! First chapters from Kathleen Cosgrove and Maxine Nunes.

Turn the page for a bonus chapter

from Michael Guillebeau's book

JOSH WHOEVER

After the Army made him a hero when he knew he wasn't, Josh just wants to stay drunk in the back of the Western World bar. But know the Russian mob thinks Josh is a detective, and the only one who can save their runaway daughter.

Library Journal said, "The collection of oddball minor characters and surprise twists deepen an already strong story. Mystery Debut of the Month."

Chapter 1

I only took this job to get fired, but now I stood here raising my hands in the air like any good citizen being robbed.

Two robbers had popped into the bank from nowhere. From inside my little bank teller window, I had no real view of them walking in the door but now they strutted around in white paper lab suits, looking like big bunny rabbits waving guns at random around the bank lobby.

The tall one did all the talking. "Open your cash drawers, put your hands in the air, and shut up."

His eyes darted from teller to teller looking for a challenge. The young girl in front of him just stood there frozen. He waved his gun at the ceiling and let off a burst and the girl screamed and opened her drawer.

"This. Is. A. Robbery." He shouted each word loud and important, like he was hyping a band at a rock concert.

Like we needed a program to tell us what's going on here. Like I needed a program to tell me that my own future was over if they got away with this robbery.

The short one reached up with the barrel of his AK-47 and pushed away the video camera over the door so that it saw only the ceiling. They started at the far end and worked their way down the long row of tellers toward me.

I stood motionless and watched, curious about how they did this. I knew plenty about small-time scams, but I'd never seen a big-time bank robbery like this before.

The tall guy did all the talking but looked at the silent one for something. There: that was it. Silent shook his head, and Tall skipped a teller. Silent knew something; he skipped the tellers with dye packs.

I admired them for pulling this off, admired the details: the paper lab suits were a good touch. No one would remember anything about the robbers except the white suits with hoods. Probably buy them cheap at some med supply place; add a white ski mask, and you can wear anything you like underneath.

Except for the shoes. Tall had flashy basketball kicks that demanded respect on the street, what you'd expect from a robber. But Silent had a pair of black Ferragamos, rich businessman shoes that cost three hundred dollars new, except his weren't new. The kind of guy who would buy these shoes wouldn't keep his shoes this long; he either had money or worked for guys with money and had to keep up. Either way, it stood out and it offended me. I was a pro in my own way. I respected pros. You've got to get the details right.

The two guys moved the same way: pro, but with a flaw. They looked casual, even random, but I could tell it was rehearsed. No one but me would remember that later, and that was good.

But the body language had a flaw. Tall moved like a bank robber in a movie, all swagger and attitude, waving the gun around and yelling at anything. Silent faded into the background and that was good, too, but the pose was wrong. He hunched over and shuffled like a kicked dog. This wasn't a man used to demanding other people's money. Silent begged people for money every day and hated doing it but had to pay the rent.

There, in a flash I had it. Silent's walk and Silent's shoes belonged to Robert, the assistant manager of the bank. I watched him get pushed around every day by the manager. Now Robert was getting his payback.

See, that was the tell, the one detail that betrayed all your hard work because it was too much a part of who you were for you to even know it was there. I knew how to stay in character and keep the game going until I got to the payoff. Even now, when I wanted to grab the guys and tell them to start over, to come through the doors this way or that, even now I just stood there impassively with my hands in the air.

I wanted to tell them: be a pro. Be a pro, or be burned.

I reached over quick and took the dye pack from Kelly's open drawer, one of the old-style packs with a timer. Kelly smiled weakly back at me, chewed her gum faster and looked away. I pressed the timer button and put it in my own drawer.

Tall came to me and waved his gun. I smiled and scooped up the cash and dye pack and shoveled them on top of the money in the bag. I felt like saying "sorry" to the big bunny rabbit, but the best I could do was apologize in my head.

Sorry, I thought, but I can't let San Francisco's finest look at the personnel records and ask me questions, the kind of questions these giant companies *should* ask before they hire someone but never do. Big dogs can't be bothered checking on the little guys who really make up their companies.

And that's why I hated these companies, hated so much of the world: be a pro, treat people and your job with respect, or get out.

Me? I got out.

Turn the page for a bonus chapter

from Michael Guillebeau's book

MAD LIBRARIAN

A Southern librarian has to fight back to save her library and her community.

PUBLISHER'S WEEKLY SAYS, "Guillebeau blends humor and mystery perfectly in this comic thriller."

2017 FOREWORD REVIEWS INDIE GOLD WINNER FOR BEST HUMOR NOVEL!

one

little pricks

SERENITY TRIED.

She tried to be a model librarian: professional, polite and as gentle-spoken on the outside as she could possibly be.

Her library was America at its best. In its public spaces, the MAD—as the librarians called the Maddington Public Library, from the abbreviation stamped on its books—was the eminently normal center of an eminently normal small Southern city. No matter what else was going on in the city outside: failing schools, drugs in the street, too few good jobs, teen-aged boys wearing their pants too low and homeless men with no pants at all—the city fathers expected Head Librarian Serenity Hammer to keep the MAD a calm oasis of normalcy as proof that the city fathers themselves were actually doing their jobs. And, they expected her to do that whether they did anything themselves or even supplied the library with actual support.

Serenity tried to live up to that, too.

Which was why, on a hot August morning, she was locked alone in a children's reading room with a coffee cup of rum for fortitude, a rat named Faulkner for company, a copy of Harper Lee's *To Kill a Mockingbird* for guidance, and a highly illegal choice before her.

Serenity Hammer was a librarian. And Serenity was mad.

• • •

TWO DAYS BEFORE she wrestled with moral dilemma, Serenity threw open the library's glass doors on a hot Wednesday morning in August. She smiled as patrons flowed past on their way to her books.

She picked up a handful of books from the "to be shelved" cart and turned to the stacks. She ran her finger along the spine of one, inhaled the paper-and-ink smell, and smiled again.

Someone screamed, “Damned stupid computers.” She put the books back on the cart.

Maybe later.

She then walked up to a worn-out older woman who was slapping a worn-out library computer like it had stole from her. Serenity took the woman’s hands away from the computer and held them.

“I knowed this was a bad idea,” the woman said. “I told my councilman I needed a job and he said they had to close the employment office and he told me to go to the library. But your damned computer just tells me what books you got here. Don’t want a book; want a job.”

The woman tried to pull her hands away but Serenity held on. The woman’s jaw was still jutting out but her eyes were full of fear and shame.

Serenity put the woman’s hands in her lap and pulled up a chair. “Then let’s find you a job. What can you do?”

“Not a goddamned thing. Forty years looking after my husband and he died. Now I don’t know what to do and they ain’t nobody to ask that won’t charge more money than I got and I just feel like everybody's letting me get torn to pieces."

"So, what have you been doing in those forty years?"

"Cooking and cleaning and raising kids and—"

"There. Know much about baking?"

"Well, of course. Who do you think made all them cupcakes the kids took to school?"

"Good." The woman slid over and Serenity brought up a web page. "There's a bakery out on Segers Road. They specialize in making treats for people who have special dietary needs. They were in here yesterday looking for a book on hiring folks."

The woman shook her finger at the screen. "They better be careful. My husband Christopher was a diabetic. There's some stuff you got to know if you're cooking for diabetics."

Serenity touched her on the shoulder. "You're just what they need. But you'll need a resume." Serenity slid back and turned the keyboard to the woman. "You type, and I'll help you."

A few minutes later, a warm sheet of paper slid out of the printer, and Serenity handed it to the woman. "Take that to Stacey out at Liberated Specialty Foods, see if you can help each other."

The woman's tears were gone, "What would we do if the library wasn't here?"

Serenity said, "My library will always—"

A blue-haired woman grabbed her elbow.

"This thing ain't got nothing in it."

She shoved a book in Serenity's hands and Serenity smiled. The woman was the wife of the Church of Christ's choir director. She had joined the Romance Book Club so she could condemn immorality. Flipping through the pages, Serenity handed the book back and pointed to the middle of a page. "Here."

The choir director's wife bobbed her head up and down like a nervous bird, studying the page and popping up to make sure no one saw her. She raised her head one last time with her mouth open.

"Praise Jesus. This is terrible."

Anything to keep them coming in.

Serenity headed for her office door. A twenty-something woman with books clutched to her chest and a librarian's badge blocked her path.

Fine. She didn't want to face what was waiting behind that door anyway.

"Ms. Hammer, he's back."

"Who?"

Amanda Doom pulled one hand from under her books and slowly raised her index finger until it was straight up. "Do you want me to get security?"

Serenity looked over at the high school boy who had volunteered to wear the red "Security" tee shirt today.

"No."

"I can call the police."

"Take them a half-hour to get here," Serenity said. "Besides, he's cousin to the wife of the district attorney. We'll just wind up in a long discussion about his constitutional rights, again. No, we need to end this once and for all. We're a library. Our power is books."

She pulled out the biggest atlas she could carry. "Keep his attention so he won't see me coming."

Serenity weaved through the stacks until she heard two teen-aged girls giggling.

"Smaller than I thought it would be," said one. More giggles.

Serenity peeked through a gap in the books and saw the back of a 1940's style trench coat. She eased her way around behind him and stepped into his aisle.

Doom was standing in front of the man as requested, looking shocked, but now she smiled at

Serenity and the surprise was gone. The trench coat spun toward her. Move fast. She opened the atlas and took one giant step forward. The opening of the trench coat rotated into view followed by the man's grinning face and his . . . pride.

Serenity slammed the heavy book shut on the man with a vengeance. He jumped and screamed and she yanked the book away with a nasty jerk.

He fell back against the stacks and put his hands over himself. "My rights."

She held the book up in both hands like Moses handing down the commandments. "Freedom of the press trumps freedom of expression." Shook it at him. "By. The. Book."

She shoved him aside.

"Come back again, Cy, and I'm going for the unabridged dictionary." The teenaged girls giggled at "dictionary." She held the book out to Doom and the girl took it like she was accepting a dead rat.

"Shelve this, please." Serenity looked back at Cy and said, "I'm tired of wasting my big books on you little pricks."

Turn the page for a bonus chapter

from Kathleen Cosgrove's book

ENGULFED

My introduction to Kathleen Cosgrove's writing came when my wife came running up from the beach with a copy of Engulfed in her hands, yelling, "You have got to read this book until page 187." She was right. Kathleen's Maggie Finn books are the funniest Florida weird mysteries out there, bar none.

CHAPTER ONE

When you're a divorced woman from an Irish Catholic home, you sort of expect God to punish you once in a while. It's his benevolent way of making you pay here, so you don't have to burn in hell later; at least that's how I look at it. Therefore, I was not really surprised when Hurricane Fanny, who was supposed to make landfall in Mexico, changed her trajectory and headed toward southwest Florida the moment my plane touched down at the Fort Myers airport. I did take exception this time since I was here to do a good deed and help my folks move into their fancy new retirement home. But, such is my relationship with The Almighty and my reason for being in a place that I consider to be only slightly more livable than the sun.

The drive to Shell Harbor Assisted living took me ten minutes and two bottled waters. By the time I got there, I was so damp from the humidity no less than two people stopped to ask if it was raining,

Before I could find a ladies room to freshen up, I heard the sound of high heels clicking down the hall and turned to see a young, attractive woman making her way to me at a near gallop speed. Her brown, shoulder length hair bounced and glistened like in a shampoo commercial; the type of woman who wouldn't sweat in a steam room, so naturally I disliked her.

"Mrs. Finn? I'm so glad you could come. I'm Brandy," she said, a bit out of breath. "I'm the director here. I met your folks, lovely couple, we're super excited they'll be living here. I know we promised you a tour this morning but since the hurricane tomorrow—well, this may not be the best time."

"I know," I said, "I think I have to go buy a flashlight or something, but I thought I'd just take a quick peek if you don't mind."

She looked at the receptionist who was giving her the wide-eyed, *please don't make me take this sweaty lady around,* look. Then she put her arm through mine like we were on a date, smiled, glanced at my hair and asked, "Is it raining?"

*****

"What's going on here?" I asked when we approached the patio. A large contingency of seniors were gathered round a group of men setting up sound equipment.

"Oh," she said, "The radio station is here today to do a live broadcast from 9:00 to 11:00. It's always so much fun when they come that we decided not to cancel. They give out prizes and the D.J. they send is so funny, Ziggy he calls himself. They all love him here, they never miss his show. I can introduce you if you'd like."

"Gee thanks, but I think I'll pass," I said. "I've still got lots of stuff to get ready at my parents' home."

I raised my voice attempting to be heard over the sound of a dozen people speaking to each other at the same level you would if you were standing in front of a jet engine.

I spotted a van parked in the circular drive that separated the building from the lake and adjacent golf course. The vehicle had a satellite dish attached to the side and a painted mural of a beach that included crabs, seagulls and a leaping dolphin, all with images of people where the animal head should be. I assumed these were the radio personalities and I recognized the *crab man* as the one seated at the long table in the center of the lobby. The call letters for the station were painted on the side of the van in large green letters—WWTF.

"The radio station is WWTF?" I asked Brandy.

"Yes, it stands for Waving Through Florida."

"But, surely they must get kid..."

Brandy interrupted me, "Oh Ziggy!" she waved to the crab man.

Ziggy stood up and made his way toward us. He was about my age, tall, thin and nice looking. He wore shorts that went mid-calf, a long sleeve *Tommy Bahama* shirt, and a leather necklace with an Indian head nickel dangling from it. I suddenly felt a little more self-conscious of my appearance and reached up to tame my hair, instantly regretting it; it looked so obvious.

"Brandy! Long time no see. How've you been darlin'?" he asked with a smile and an arm around her shoulder.

"Hi Ziggy," Brandy gushed. "It's really great you're here. Everyone's been asking when you were coming back."

He looked at me and smiled.

"Ziggy, this is Mrs. Finn." Brandy said. "Her parents are moving in the beginning of the month."

"Maggie," I said as I shook his hand, "nice to meet you."

"Nice to meet you Maggie," he said. "This joint is pretty nice huh? If I weren't so young, I'd be looking at moving in myself."

"Well, it's very nice to meet you too," I said. "Brandy says you're quite a hit here at The Shell."

"Ah, yeah, they love me here, they're my best audience. All the markets I've worked in, this is definitely my favorite."

He looked around and waved at a couple of elderly women who giggled and waved back.

I really lucked out getting this gig," he continued, "great folks down here. Yep, I love it."

He stopped himself, probably aware that he was going too far out of his way to sound convincing, but I think Brandy, at least, was buying it. From the tattoos and long hair I was certain he was more used to playing Pearl Jam than String of Pearls.

"You gonna stick around and watch the show?" he asked. "We have a lot of fun and some company's comin' out later to demo a new mobility device."

"Gee, that does sound fun," I said, more sarcastically than I had wanted, "but I've got an appointment."

"Suit yourself," he said, and looked at his audience. "I gotta get back to work."

He sauntered back to his table in long, easy strides and began talking to one of the set up crew.

"I think I insulted him," I told Brandy, "I didn't really mean it like that."

"Oh, I'm sure he wasn't insulted, he says crazy things himself all the time."

On our walk back Brandy stopped suddenly and yelled, "Jesus!"

I don't know if I was more surprised by her sudden outburst or the fact that she was cursing.

"Jesus," she hollered again, and a man hurried over to us.

"Si Miss Brandi?"

"Jesus, there's a raccoon in the bird bath again, take him away, quickly!" she said in a tone more suited to an impending avalanche.

The animal had something it was tossing about that looked like a small bone. "It looks kind of cute," I said, "look, it's washing its food in the water."

We watched as Jesus approached the animal stealthily, looking at it, then back at us, then at the animal again. When he got within five feet of it the raccoon tossed the bone at Jesus and ran across the lawn into the brush near the lake. I stopped watching the animal when I heard Jesus let out a blood curdling scream.

By the time Brandy and I reached him he was staring at the ground mumbling in Spanish and crossing himself.

"Jesus," I said, "I could be wrong, but that sure does look like a man's..."

"Si," agreed Jesus, "a pene."

"Yep," I said, "that's a pene alright. And if there's a pene here," I pointed at the object, "then there must be…"

Brandy looked at the thing, stood motionless for a minute as though someone had hit the pause button on the remote, and then fainted.

"Someone call a doctor!" I yelled.

A cleaning lady came over with a bottle of Windex, waving it under Brandy's nose.

Someone tapped me on the shoulder. I jumped and turned to see one of the landscapers holding a leaf bag out to me. He said something in Spanish that sounded like a question.

"Does anyone here speak Spanish?" I asked the crowd.

One of the women, part of the kitchen staff, came over and said something to him in Spanish, he replied in the same language. She turned to me and said, "He wants to know what he should do with this."

The man held up the bag.

"What's in it?" I asked.

"A leg," she said, dramatically in her heavy Cuban accent.

"Si, leg," the man said.

I looked in the bag, felt woozy and yelled, "Someone bring me the Windex!"

Turn the page for a bonus chapter

from Maxine Nunes book

DAZZLED

If you want the dark underbelly of Hollywood glamor, vividly written, Maxine Nunes is the writer for you.

CHAPTER 1

What's real? Darla used to ask me. *How do you know what's real?* I never understood the question. But then I didn't have platinum hair and cheekbones that could cut glass, and no one ever offered to buy me a Rolls if I spent one night naked in his bed. Darla was a brilliant neon sign flashing pure escape. You almost didn't notice that those lovely green eyes didn't blaze like the rest of her. She was both main attraction and sad observer at the carnival. Something had damaged her at a very young age. We never talked much about it, but we recognized this in each other from the start. Isn't that what friendship is?

The week she disappeared was as extreme as she was. Triple-digit heat in late August and wavy layers of smog suffocating the city. By ten in the morning, it was brutal everywhere, and on the sidewalks in front of the homeless shelter, with the sun bouncing off the film crew trailers and the odor of unwashed bodies and general decay, it was a very special episode of hell. Beneath an archway, a tall man with a filthy blanket draped over his head rolled his eyes heavenward like a biblical prophet. Or a *Star Trek* castaway waiting to be beamed up.

In one of those trailers, where air conditioning brought the temperature down to the high nineties, I was being stuffed into a fitted leather jacket two sizes too small. Perspiration had already ruined my makeup and the dark circles under my eyes were starting to show through.

Heat keeping you up, hon? the makeup girl had asked. I'd nodded. Half the truth.

Mykel Z, the costume designer, was trying to zip me into the jacket, but his fingers were sweating and frustrating his attempts. "If you'd get yourself boobs, Nikki," he said, "we wouldn't have to squeeze you into size zero to work up a little cleavage."

"Bigger boobs for you, smaller nose for my agent. Average it out and I'm perfect."

"Almost. Legs from here to eternity, long dark hair to die for. But the nose *is* a bit roller derby, darling. Did you break it?"

"When I was a kid."

"I'll give you the name of a marvelous doctor, a genius with noses. And his lifts for my older ladies . . . I swear the seams don't even show."

"I'm not sure I want to wake up one morning and see someone else in the mirror."

"An idealist. Good luck, honey."

I was used to this. At my first Hollywood party, a guy asked me what I did. When I told him, he looked bewildered. Then he brightened. "Oh," he said, "I guess you could play a real person."

Outside, a prop guy was spraying a couple of shopping carts to dull down their newness, and a wardrobe assistant walked a few extras onto the set.

"No, no, no!" Mykel cried, running out the door, letting in a flush of hot air. "Layers! They need layers!" With a broad motion of his arm, he pointed to some people in the little park on the corner. "Use your eyes! The homeless *totally* invented layering!"

I took advantage of the break, managed to find my phone in the junk shop that is my shoulder bag, and called Darla's cell again. It flipped straight over to her voice mail. Like it had for three days, since this shoot had begun. No point leaving another message.

Mykel flew back into the trailer and stared at me for a few seconds, blinked like he was fighting back tears, then began to tackle the zipper again.

It moved up an inch before it caught on the leather.

He dropped his arms, his lips trembled, then he opened the trailer door again and stuck his head out.

"*Benito*!" he hollered, with an edge of real panic in his voice. When Benito, his "shlepper," did not appear, Mykel flopped down on a chair and blotted his face with a tissue.

"Where the hell has he gone?"

"You sent him for a Frappuccino," I said.

"Ten minutes ago!"

"It's hard to find a decent barista on Skid Row, Mykel."

"Maybe that's why these people look so depressed."

"You know what," I said, "let's forget the jacket for a while. They're nowhere near ready to shoot. I'm gonna grab some water from the fridge. Want a bottle?"

"Thank you, sweetie." Mykel placed the jacket back on its hanger with all the tenderness due a garment that cost more than I was being paid for a week's work.

Beneath my tank top, a trickle of sweat from my bra reminded me I was still padded with chicken cutlets—the silicone inserts the director wanted for every female in the cast over the age of twelve. When I removed them, I felt almost human again.

Outside, an assistant was trying to wrangle the extras—a task that had turned chaotic, since real street people kept slipping past security to get to the bagel table. But even from this distance, it was easy to tell them apart. You only had to look at their faces. On some, the flesh itself was infused with misery, the eyes dazed with hopelessness. The rest, in the same soiled layers, were radiant and eager to be noticed.

I'd had a taste of both, but a year on the streets at fifteen had been enough. I got a false ID, found jobs, and managed to take care of myself. But there was something restless in me and I never stayed in one place too long. Somehow, more than a decade slipped by. And what had seemed like freedom began to close in on me.

Then I wound up in L.A. and started picking up rent money working as an extra. A crime show was shooting a Manhattan street scene in downtown Los Angeles, and I got pulled out of the crowd because of my "New York face" for a line they had added: *Ain't seen her in a long time, mistah.* That amazing stroke of luck—and the three-thousand dollar initiation fee I was still paying off—got me my union card.

Now I had pictures and an agent and classes, and that was what really hooked me. Acting may be make believe, but in class the truth beneath the face you showed the world was not only welcome but demanded.

Only that wasn't exactly what working as an actor was like.

This job was a midseason pilot called *Street*, a "fish out of water" comedy about three girls from Beverly Hills who start a gourmet soup kitchen for the homeless. "*Clueless* meets *Pursuit of Happyness*" is how my agent described it. My role—two days' work that could "go to semi-recurring"—was as a homeless person who gets a makeover.

A wave of hot air blew into the trailer, followed by the production assistant, who looked at me and let out a shriek.

"*Mykel!* Why isn't she in costume? They're *ready* for her."

And they were.

Four hours later.

* * *

By the time they released me it was past ten, and as the crew struck the lights and equipment, the homeless began crawling into makeshift tents of newspapers and old blankets and cartons, or gathering in doorways, palming small packets that would get them through the night.

Hot stale air still hung over the city as I walked to my car, an ancient MGB that looked right at home in its own version of layers—black over Haight-Ashbury psychedelic over the original British racing green. The standard joke about MGs is that you share custody with your mechanic, but someone had replaced the temperamental English parts with American ones, and it actually started up every time I turned the ignition key.

With the top down, the hot Santa Anas were better than no breeze at all as I passed the rolling lawns and swaying palms of MacArthur Park, moonlight dusting the lake and the silhouetted figures of dealers and users.

A half hour later, I turned onto La Cienega and headed north past the cool stone facades of restaurant row, past Beverly Center whose colored lights bounced off gleaming Mercedes, Lexus SUVs and the occasional virtuous Prius, past the mansard-roofed Sofitel, past the crowds milling outside a few nightspots.

My little cottage still held all the heat of the day. I stripped down to panties, then finished off a pint of Chunky Monkey— ate it straight from the carton in a current of cold air from the open fridge door—and dragged myself into the bedroom.

I used up all the cool spots on the sheet in about five minutes and picked up a mystery from the night table. But no matter how hunky the hero, an old paperback cannot fill the other side of the bed, and I started to think about the man who'd occupied that space until a couple of weeks ago. Dan Ackerman. A good, solid guy, and I left him . . . why? Maybe because he was a good, solid guy.

The only other person in my life who mattered was Darla, and she hadn't returned my calls, which really wasn't like her at all. Even when she was on location, she'd phone and talk about anything—what they had for lunch, how filthy the honey wagons got—just to keep from feeling lonely.

I wondered if she was mad at me, if maybe I shouldn't have been so blunt about her ex-boyfriend Jimmy. It was past midnight and too late to call. But I sent a quick text, then found myself listening in the silence for the phone to chime with her answer.

I turned on the TV. Fourteen dead in the Middle East and four dead in a murder in the Hollywood Hills. But no worries. Just wait for election day. Mike Ryle, TV Land western star/turned senate candidate, was saying, "Let's return to the America I grew up in." He sounded so earnest, you could almost forget that he'd grown up in the America of Vietnam and segregation and backstreet abortions.

When the infomercials started, I flicked the TV off and watched the minutes and the hours on the clock change. As the city was waking up, I fell asleep.

Made in the USA
Columbia, SC
17 October 2020